Voices In My Head

Susan Lynn Solomon

ALL RIGHTS RESERVED

Cover Art:
Michelle Crocker

http://mlcdesigns4you.weebly.com/

Publisher's Note:

This is a work of fiction. All names, characters, places, and events are the work of the author's imagination.

Any resemblance to real persons, places, or events is coincidental.

Solstice Publishing - www.solsticepublishing.com

Voices in My Head
Susan Lynn Solomon

Dedication

For Corey, Shelby and Travis
My family, my joy

Foreword

Susan Lynn Solomon is a writer's writer.

Suzy, as she is known to her friends, is a person driven by an inescapable need to tell stories. She can no more give up imagining characters and circumstances than she can give up air or food. She writes at a furious rate, producing novels and stories that captivate and delight. Her imagination is what sustains her, and we, her readers, are the better for her obsession.

Like all gifted writers, Susan is a universalist, unburdened by the curse of being able to tell only one kind of story. She gets an idea, then decides upon the best way to discharge that idea, the best characters, the best settings, and the best narrative voice to attain maximum effect. If reading is a way to slip into other times and places and faces from the relative comfort of an armchair, she is a devilishly clever tour guide who can take you to surprising places and surprising connections. In the nine tales in this book, she dazzles us with journeys into the unexpected and its impact on people we feel we already know.

War? In *Mystery of the Carousel*, she explores the link between a veteran of the Great War and the carousel on which, as a child, he imagined great battles. Incest? Where better to explore its devastations than early 19th Century England in *Maggie's End*? Magic? *Witches Gumbo* takes us to Bayou LaFit and a powerful comeuppance. Mystery? Try *The Holmes Society* for a new take on amateur sleuthing. Death? *Kaddish* shows the unavoidable bond between death and identity.

In these and the other stories that comprise the voices in her head, Susan Lynn Solomon opens our minds, and the rhythm of our lives, to the voices in her heart. Enjoy.

Gary Earl Ross
Professor Emeritus, University at Buffalo
Author of Nickel City Blues and The Mark of Cain

Mystery of the Carousel

August 1918. Recently returned from France, Tom Ryan struggles with the reality of The Great War... The War to End All Wars. The experience was not the heroic enterprise he and his friends dreamed of when, as children, they rode off to battle on carousel horses.

Carousel on a hill, bound in weeds,
neglected, decrepit. Do you remember
it was painted, you were young,
and its chargers bore you gaily off to war?
Listen to the wind sing,
a calliope with fifes and bells.
Squint your eyes, you might see
the child you were on that carousel.

August 1918. Paddy's Pub was dim that sultry night. Fans overhead whirred in a slow rhythm. Six silent patrons on stools spaced along the bar, stared bleary-eyed into the mirror or into their shot glasses. Tom Ryan slouched at the far end, conversing with his drink. He rarely sat anymore. His glass grasped in both hands, he gulped a greedy swallow. As he held the glass out for another refill, a boreal wind slapped slats of loose lumber from the side wall of Westra's Dairy across the street. The wood toppled onto the hitch of a gig in the yard, then scattered across the cobblestones on Oliver Street. Startled, the horse team pulling Wattengel's black carriage back to the stable behind his Funeral Home, reared, and bolted. Hooves clopped. Whinnying, the horses bounced the carriage off the curb.

Ryan's glass clattered on the floor. He shrank back against the mahogany bar, his haunted eyes searching the corners of the room.

"What's the matter, lad?" Paddy asked.

Ryan peered up at the hammered tin ceiling, bracing himself for the shattering blast he feared would surely follow. When the street again fell silent, he made a vague attempt to tuck his stained shirt into his trousers, and began to pace. Back and forth he went across the scuffed plank floor, twenty strides from the narrow window in front to the arch of the back room where two pool players in overalls silently went about their game.

"Gotta be careful every minute," Ryan mumbled.

As if they were Hun troops placed to block his escape, he smacked chairs from his path.

"Just Ryan being Ryan," Paddy commented to a man whose head was bent over his beer.

The man shrugged.

George McGuire, a hefty bargeman, lifted his shaggy head from the bar. "Sit still a minute, would ya," he groaned at the pacer's back. "Bouncin' 'round like that, you're makin' me nuts."

Ryan grunted.

"Whadya say?" McGuire sat up straight.

The pacing stopped. Ryan's lean body tensed. He brushed a hand across the skin of his scalp. He'd shaved his head in the trench after a fateful day in France. "Didn't say nothing," he grumbled. "Go back to sleeping in your beer."

"You did!" McGuire clenched his fist. "Heard you call me somethin'."

In a swift motion, Paddy grabbed the fist from across the bar. "Boys, boys, it's too hot a night for arguing," he said. "'Sides, he wasn't talking to you, George."

"Who then?" McGuire's brow furrowed as he glared over his shoulder.

At the window, Ryan stared down the street toward Palmer's Hardware Store, hearing, yet not listening to the barkeeper and the bargeman. Though his lips moved, he spoke no words.

Paddy followed the young man's gaze. "Dunno," he said. "Maybe to Nick Bodoni—used to clerk down at Palmer's. You remember him, don't you, George?"

McGuire scowled.

"Sure you do. Him and Ryan were friends forever. Signed up together to fight with the Fifth in France." The barkeeper shook his head and wiped his hands on his apron.

"Good boy, he was, that Nick. Pity 'bout him. Buried somewhere in France I hear—not enough of him left to send home. His ma still cries over losing him."

As if assailed by a ghost, Ryan shivered.

His eyes flicking toward the window, Paddy said, "I hear Ryan was right there when the shell exploded. Took Nick, Charlie Brookes, half his unit in one blast. Maybe it's them he's talking to."

"What do you know about it?" Ryan spun to McGuire. His blue eyes burning with the fire of war, he snarled, "What do any of you know about any of it? Sitting safe, comfortable back here while we—"

Paddy pounded a glass on the bar, and poured a shot. "C'mon, boyo, have another one on me."

Ryan snatched up the glass and raised it in a salute. "Here's to them times Nick, and me, and Charlie was kids out to the fair by Crystal Beach. Band organ music from the carousel sounding like a circus parade... so loud you could hear it clear 'cross Lake Erie. Made us wanna run, ride on it, dream 'bout being cavalry soldiers. Yeah, soldiers... Shit, we was just kids, what'd we know? What'd any of us..."

Downing the whisky, he turned a neat about-face. Once more at the window, his voice faded to someplace in the past.

"See, he's just hurting a bit," Paddy said to McGuire. "Go easy on the lad."

His back stiff, Ryan muttered, "Sure, go ahead, be easy on the poor lad. Came back broken, so pity him. Damn you all for being safe back here while we're muddy in foxholes facing the Hun. Damn cowards!"

"Yellow, am I?" McGuire jumped from his stool and barged after Ryan.

Paddy moved from behind the bar faster than anyone might have though a man of his size was capable. "That's not a thing to be saying, Tom. George here would've gone with you. Tried to sign up, but he was too old. You know that."

"Yeah, I know a lotta things. Too many things—" Ryan rubbed a sleeve roughly across his eyes. "Like maybe damn George could've tried harder."

The barman grabbed Ryan's shoulders and turned him around. "You've had too much, lad. Go home, sleep it off," he said as he shoved him out the door.

Ryan staggered into the shadows. For a moment, he stopped outside another of the hundred bars along Oliver Street. Rubbing his forehead, he gazed through the filigreed words on the window.

Maybe one more before…

He patted his pocket, hearing only the thin jingle of a few small coins. In his jacket was the tin flask he carried for emergencies like this. There wasn't much whisky in it, but maybe enough to dull the cries echoing day and night; maybe enough so he could sleep without cringing in bed.

***

In the middle of that night, flask in hand, Ryan slouched along the New York Central tracks in the downtown business district. The streets were deserted, stores locked, windows shuttered. Four-story buildings with wood facades loomed over him like dark spirits.

The tracks rattled as the 2:35 freight raced up the line. Ryan hopped on a rail. One foot in front of the other, arms out, he balanced like the daredevil he'd once seen walk a tightrope across the Niagara Gorge.

Hang on here a mite longer, he thought, *engine'll do me.*

The train was almost on him, its shrill whistle like the one his colonel blew in France just before they went over the top. In a move the army had drilled into him until it was instinct, he jumped aside and barrel-rolled. As the iron monster roared past, he rose unsteadily and smacked the dust from his jacket.

"Can't even do this right, Ryan," he moaned. "Got no nerve anymore."

Soon his footsteps echoed on the wood planks of a bridge arching over the Erie Barge Canal. Water lapped at its stanchions and along the stone banks. He halted in the center where moonlight peeked over a row of warehouses.

"I'm sorry," he groaned. "Nick, Charlie, I'm so—"

Something below caught his attention: had his friends come back as stars shimming on the water? He stretched far over the rail to grab for one, but was just short of drunk enough to dive for it.

In an instant, his head came up. Grasping the rail, he slowly turned. Had someone called to him? Who was singing?

The sound repeated in the distance.

His eyes darted. No one was there. Must have been a trick of the night. With a shrug, he turned a tipsy pirouette. Again he wandered off.

After ten minutes, he was lost in a black stand of massive oaks near a rise. In the center was a two-story wood structure. The roundhouse attached to it looked like a stubbed, swollen silo. To Ryan, the building seemed a distorted version of the barn it had once been. *Home of Herschell's Carousels & Amusements* was painted in tall white script above the doors. The place had been deserted since the Great War began, and to the whistle of fifes and cheers of young girls, the men who worked here sailed off.

What drew him there? Ryan wondered. His mind clouded, his thoughts jumbled, he fought to recall what happened on the bridge. He'd been working up the courage for a dive into the canal. What had stopped him? A voice. Yes, that was it—a voice. It called to him in a whisper that seemed to grow from the notes of a band organ. The ghostly melody had lured him from the canal, and it was as if he'd followed it down the dark streets. Now, standing at the base of the factory where those organs had been made, he was held in place by a single thought: he needed to ride a carousel just once more before he joined his friends.

"Dum-dum-ditty-ditty-dum…" The tune he hummed was a yearning sigh, a song the carousel at Crystal Beach had played when he, and Nick, and Charlie were kids. A hundred years ago when they were kids. Where did the music come from?

He circled the building, feeling more desperate by the minute. The melody faded. In the silence, he turned away. Then it began again, louder now. The gnarled fingers of memory grabbed his heart and pulled him to the boarded-up window of the roundhouse. The music came from in there!

As he peered through a knothole, he recalled a day he, and Nick, and Charlie had watched through this window, awestruck, while a carousel was nailed together in the roundhouse. A workman had called them inside—to test it out, the man said. There'd been no need to ask twice. They had clambered through the window and climbed aboard the tallest horses. While the carousel spun, they were the Three Musketeers riding off to save France. Brandishing imaginary swords and nattering about how someday they'd do it for real, they were lost in images of the feats they'd perform.

Now outside the roundhouse, running a hand over his scalp Ryan fought back tears for his friends, for himself, for every one of their childhood days. "Dum-dum-ditty-ditty," he hummed, then bit down on his lip.

When he leaned close for another glimpse of the memory dwelling inside, a blast of wind rattled a plank on the door.

He yanked at it. "Ow. Shit!" He jumped back, shaking off the sting of a long scrape on the back of his hand.

"This's crazy," he slurred. "What'm I doin' here? Paddy's right. Drank too much." He stumbled toward the street.

"Giving up so easy?" a voice called in the night.

He jerked around. All he could see was the army of trees surrounding the hill.

"Easy to just give up," the voice taunted.

"Who are you?" Ryan demanded. He staggered a complete circle. "Where are you?" He clenched his fists. "C'mon show yourself, you wanna fight!"

A response swelled from the organ's moan: "Don't need to fight you, Tom, you're fighting yourself. That's as much as any man can take on."

He held his ears, but could quiet neither the music nor the voice.

"Go on, go home. Give up. Easier that way," the voice said.

His head back, Ryan demanded of the sky, "What else can I do? Ain't nothin' left!"

"Quit now, you'll never know…" The words faded into a faint hum of music from inside the roundhouse.

Dum-dum-ditty…

"I'm dead. This is hell!" he cried.

Instead of running to Paddy's to hide inside another drink, he spun to the roundhouse door, and pried at the loose board. His back arched, he put his full weight into one final yank. The nails made a deep groan. The board moved enough to leave a narrow a gap.

***

𝒟ust thrown up when he slipped inside made him cough. Silken cobwebs stretched across each corner and draped over sawhorses. They glittered like jewels on abandoned blocks of wood. Shadows in improbable shapes cluttered the empty roundhouse. After a quick glance, he backed up until he hit a wall.

"What am I doing, breaking in here?" Ryan muttered. Strangely, his words weren't slurred, nor did he stumble drunkenly with each step. "That's about enough nonsense for one night. Going home."

As he turned to leave he heard a series of clicks, and the roundhouse lit in a carnival glare.

"Well, well, made it at last," the voice that had taunted him said. "Been waiting for you. Knew you'd get here sooner or later."

A slight man in oil-stained overalls stepped from a shadow. Though the rolled-up sleeves of his denim shirt revealed sinuous arms, which were young and toned, beneath a mane of white hair, the man's face was so deeply lined he might have been around since time began. As he moved closer, shadows behind him parted like curtains on a stage when a show begins.

Ryan stared past the old man. "What's this?"

The man dropped the wrench he carried into a loop on his overalls. Wiping his hands up and down his pant legs, he said, "What do you think it is?" He took Ryan's arm and steered him towards the glittering carousel that now filled the roundhouse.

The carousel's frame looked like a circus tent with its sides tied up by a rainbow of ribbons. Masks of comedy and tragedy hung between framed mirrors along the marquee's scalloped edge. Brass rods rose ten feet from a plank ring. Overhead, red and green stripes tapered up to a flag-draped center pole. On the floor in the center was a band organ: a bass drum, a keyboard, gleaming pipes shooting like skyrockets from a wood cabinet. *Dum-dum-ditty...*

The music came from that.

"It's a dream, that's what," Ryan mumbled. "Can't be nothing but a dream."

"You sure?" the man asked.

Ryan struggled to recall what he'd done that night, where he'd been. There was the argument at Paddy's, the train, the canal. Stars on the water reminded him of his lost friends—what they looked like after the stars exploded. He shoved the memory aside, replacing it with hope: maybe he *had* fallen into the canal, and this was how being dead felt. Was this what Nick and Charlie felt?

As if he'd read Ryan's mind, the old man asked, "Do you really think that's it?"

Pulling at his face, Ryan moaned, "Has to be." While he tried to wrap his mind around the idea of his own demise, he felt a sting on the back of his hand. He held it out and examined his wrist. A trickle of blood ran from the scrape left by the wood slats. "Wait a minute. You don't bleed when you're dead."

Though his smile stayed warm, the man's old eyes clouded with what might have been sorrow. "Not when the body dies," he said.

Ryan patted his arms and chest. "Not dead then," he said with no sense of relief. "I'm really here talking to you. But... who are you? What're you doing here? Why'd you call me? This place has been shut up since—"

"Slow down, boy. One thing at a time." The man laughed. "You can call me Gideon—most folks do. I'm always around, a... caretaker of sorts."

"You're here alone?"

"Not really." Gideon looked around, as if he saw others with them in the roundhouse. Ryan looked, too. He saw no one.

"Sometimes folks drop by for a visit," the old man said, as though it was a fact Ryan should know.

"Folks? What folks?"

The caretaker surrounded the question. "Simple souls mostly. Most are, you know. That's because even after a man's grown there's still something of a child in him. But you—" He chewed at his lip. "You're like this carousel over here. It'll take some work to bring the memory of it back. Might be able to do it—if the parts aren't too rusted."

"I don't understand!"

Gideon's voice was gentle. "No, don't expect you do. Leastwise, not yet. That's how it always is."

"What is?"

"All in good time, lad," Gideon said. Again he took the young man's arm.

At the old man's touch, Ryan's shoulders slumped. The ringing pain in his head withered to a vague recollection. Fear, need, even curiosity, flowed out of him until he was lost in perfect forgetfulness. He nodded at the carousel.

"That's a fine looking machine."

As if on cue, lights flickered. The band organ sang a loud fanfare.

"It is indeed." Gideon's voice carried above the organ's blare. "It's waiting for you to try out. Remember, Tom, how it used to be long ago when you watched these being built?"

At the moment the idea of riding the gleaming machine—the childishness of such an act—didn't feel absurd. Ryan grabbed a brass pole and stepped onto the platform.

Gideon threw a lever, then gave a knotted bell cord two tugs.

"Better get settled," he called. "This thing starts up pretty fast."

Ryan walked the platform, stroking each of the large horses. Frozen in mid-stride, it appeared as though only a spark were needed to send the steeds off at a gallop. Hoisting himself onto an ebony charger, he said, "Kind of strange to be riding this myself."

"There'll be others," Gideon said.

"What others?" Ryan asked, suspicion leaking in.

The old man smiled. He clanged the bell twice more, then pulled back the lever. Gears ground. With a jerk, the carousel began to move. Music from the band organ filled the roundhouse. Gideon waived his wrench like a conductor's wand. As if they were a movement in the symphony of sound, two young men ran from a dark passage behind him.

"Thought we was gonna miss this," one said. He shoved his friend, and laughed.

Out of breath, the second said, "Nah. No way it's gonna start without us."

They scrambled onto horses on either side of the black charger.

"Nick? Charlie?" Ryan gasped with a mixture of joy and shock. They were far younger than the last time he'd seen them whole in a bomb-cratered field. Their faces brought back memories no amount of liquor could dull: *the smell of sulfur and mildew; the itch of olive-drab flannel forever drenched by the mud they bellied through; barbed wire tearing at his fingers while he held it up for his friends to slither under. The wire tangled on his clothes, pinned him to the ground, left him screaming after them until he was hoarse—*

Tears held back until they burned, strained to burst through. But by now the dam was too strongly built. "Can't be you." Ryan choked on the words. "You're... both of you... over there—"

"Nah. We ain't dead," Nick said. "Not yet anyways." He ran a hand through curly dark hair, slowly, deliberately, and looked to the distance as if he could see that future time.

"Yeah," Charlie said. His fair, freckled face broke into an impish grin. "Do we look old enough to join the army?"

Ryan brushed mist from his eyes. "This can't be. You're only—"

"Kids?" Nick finished his sentence as he always had. "Damn right we are. And we're gonna have us some fun today. Right, Charlie?" His smile crinkled his eyes, and revealed a gap between his front teeth. To Ryan, he said, "Hey, stop looking at me like Mrs. Myer's old hound. It's summer. We're goin' out by Crystal Beach. Got a whole day to raise us some hell."

Ryan turned toward the shadows to hide the flask he pulled from his pocket. "I... no... can't do this. Gideon, please—"

"What's that, hooch?" Charlie reached for the flask.

"Hey, hey! You know what your old man says 'bout that stuff." Nick grabbed the flask from Charlie's hand, capped it, and shoved it back into Ryan's jacket. "He'll paddle you good, you come home smelling of it. Right, Tommy? Remember the time out behind Charlie's barn when his old man caught us?"

A smile turned up the corners of Ryan's mouth. It was quickly gone.

"Don't wanna remember that," he muttered. "Don't wanna remember anything. Gideon!"

"Can't hide from what was," the old caretaker called out. "Look at your friends. Look at them!"

It was as if some force twisted Ryan's head until he had no choice. He pinched his eyes closed. It was no use. The same force pulled his hand away and pried his eyes open. When he saw Nick's grin and heard Charlie laugh, his tense grip on the carousel horse loosened. Everything around them became a blur. While his eyes were locked on his friends, the calendar seemed to slip into reverse. He was one of The Musketeers again, carefree as he and his friends had once been. All thoughts of what had happened since faded into the shadows.

Like a wonder wheel, the carousel spun in dizzying turns. The roundhouse walls became transparent, faded. It was mid-afternoon, a warm sun high overhead. Laughter and shrieks of joy rose from the ground. The smell of cotton candy permeated the carnival air. Down the midway to Lake Erie's shore, a crowd of men and women in bright summer costumes talked nineteen to the dozen as they strolled. Children circled their legs. A gaggle of fair-goers leapt aboard each time the carousel slowed. Gideon now appeared as a young roustabout, shouting, "Still plenty of room to ride. Only a nickel—one shiny half-dime. Step right up for the thrill of your life."

Nick slid low on his horse's neck and grinned at Ryan. "Hey, remember them girls we met here last summer, out from Rochester?"

Ryan certainly did. Sisters, and all three pretty. They'd spent the day flirting with them on the beach. In a flash, the memory flew across his mind.

Wonder what they look like now. Grown up, got kids of their own?

While Ryan calculated whether the war would still rage when those kids grew up, Charlie broke into his thoughts.

"Coming back tomorrow?"

"Too much to do in the morning at the hardware store," Nick said before Ryan could answer. "Then I'm going up to Hershell's factory. Gonna learn to carve these horses. You guys wanna come?"

Charlie shook his head. "Nah. We got a baseball game in the afternoon—playing some guys from Niagara Falls."

"Hey, I'm playing, too," Ryan said. "Can't have the game without your first baseman. Remember the last time we played them? Gosh darn, Nick, that homer you hit almost reached the river."

While the carousel turned its circle of dreams, they talked until their shared memories were depleted.

When they grew quiet, Ryan said, "Hey, look at me." He grabbed the reins and kicked at the wooden underside of his horse. "I'm a Musketeer charging out to battle the British."

Charlie brandished a pocket-knife. "Me too! Got my sword right here."

"Yeah. Gonna go to war..." Nick's words trailed off. His voice held no joy.

The sun slipped from the sky. The carousel slowed. The crowd was gone. They were back inside the roundhouse walls.

Nick slid from his horse and yawned. "What a great day."

"No! Don't leave. Not yet!" Ryan shouted.

"Sorry, Tommy," Charlie said. "We gotta get to work." He hiked the back of hand-me-down pants that were a size too big. His head low, he plodded toward the dark passage.

The band organ faded to a distant hum.

Ryan cried, "Stay! Please... there's so much—" He jumped from his horse. "Wait—" He pulled the tin flask from his pocket and took a swig.

Gideon glanced at Nick. "I hoped another day with you boys would help some." He laid his wrench against the carousel's gears. "Needs another adjustment."

Caressing his flask as if it were a lover, Ryan thought, *Don't need nothing but this to fix me.*

Just short of the passage, Nick glanced over his shoulder at Gideon. "Might help if you put him to work, learn 'em a thing or three in the shop."

As soon as those words were out, time and Nick and Charlie froze.

Gideon looked up to the roundhouse roof, then at Ryan sipping from his flask.

"Maybe. Could work—" After what might have been five minutes, he said, "Go with them, lad."

As if freed by the words, Charlie ran into the passage. Nick charged after him. Ryan slugged another swallow from his flask, and slowly followed.

***

The passage opened into a narrow space, heavy with the musty odor of long disuse. As Ryan edged into it, he felt as though he walked on gravel or maybe sand—in the dim light that looked as though it broke through an evening fog, he couldn't tell. Unable to determine where the walls met the floor, he wasn't certain if this even was a room. He turned back to look at where he'd come from. There was no doorway. While he struggled for a grip on where he was, he heard echoed whispers from behind. Again he turned, leaned forward, and peered into the fog. No one was in the room—if it was a room—except his two friends and a wiry, hawk-nosed man they talked to.

"Tommy, come over here," Charlie said. Nick waived him over.

He held back, pulling at his trousers.

"Come here." Nick grabbed Ryan's sleeve and pulled him toward hawk-nose. "This here's Mr. Nathanial," he said. "He's foreman of the paint shop,"

Though Ryan stood beside Nick, it sounded as though his voice came from a distance.

"Mr. Nate," Charlie said, "this here's Tom Ryan, a pal of ours. Gideon says to have 'im work in the shop a while."

The foreman ran a hand along his long red beard. "Don't know. Got enough to worry on without his kind of problem."

"Nate!" Gideon's voice boomed down from what now appeared to be a ceiling above them.

Ryan swung his head around. Gideon wasn't in the room.

The foreman shrugged. "Guess it don't take much to use a primer brush." Taking Ryan's arm, he called out, "Raphael, got a new boy here. Get him into overalls. Set him up where you can keep an eye on him."

Ryan twisted his body, but couldn't find who hawk-nose had spoken to. When he turned back, a lanky man with a long neck and a crop of black hair stood at Nathaniel's side. Resting the long fingers of a delicate hand on Ryan's shoulder, he said, "Sure thing, Mr. Nate. We could use the help since Jeremy moved on."

Raphael was shorter than the others, dark skinned—Spanish maybe, or Portuguese, Ryan thought. With the war on, Iberian crews worked the canal and Lake Erie docks.

With a slight accent the man said, "C'mon with me. I'll show you what to do." His Adam's apple bobbed up and down when he spoke.

Ryan wanted to tell Nick he wouldn't paint with a primer brush, didn't want to work in this place. Didn't want to work anywhere. He craned his neck to tell Nick and Charlie and the foreman thanks, but he was going back to Paddy's.

They weren't there.

The dark-skinned man slapped his knee and laughed. "Oughta see your face." He shook his head, laughed again. Still shaking his head, he took Ryan's elbow.

As if this were a cue it awaited, the fog dissipated.

They now stood in the center of a long, narrow room, which was alive with color. Around them, a dozen brush-wielding men called to each other. Their voices bounced from the walls to the low ceiling.

Ryan gasped. It was as if the room and the men had been there all along, but he hadn't been able to see them.

"They're putting on the undercoat," Raphael explained. He pointed around at workers who brushed dull white paint onto a herd of wooden horses. "Those over there are enameling the primed bodies." Again he pointed, this time at two men who carefully tinted the illusion of muscle tone on the animals. "Those ones are artists." He lifted his nose with a finger, as if to imply they thought they were better than the rest. "When they're done doing that, they'll paint the saddles and tack."

While Ryan stood as still as one of the horses, straining to take in what he saw, Raphael dipped a brush in a pot, which seemed to have materialized at his feet. He shoved the handle into Ryan's hand, and said, "First thing, gotta lay on five coats of this white primer."

The weight of the brush was as unexpected as everything had been since Ryan broke into the roundhouse. His arm was yanked down, the brush slapped his side.

"Hey, this coat's the only one I got," he complained. The brush clattered on floor when he released it to assess the damage. "What the... how'd I get into these?" He was dressed in overalls like everyone else.

"Gotta stop fighting it—gets easier after a bit," Raphael said as he stooped to pick up the brush.

Ryan rubbed his eyes. Voices of people who weren't there; others who'd materialized in the mist; friends alive when they couldn't be; his familiar clothes changed: Paddy must've poured him some real bad hooch. He hoped that was it, because if he wasn't rot-gut sick— Well, he'd heard about the Buffalo Lunatic Asylum.

"Gonna stand there gawking the day away, or make yourself useful?" Raphael grumbled. The other workers laughed.

His face growing warm from embarrassment, Ryan hefted the large brush, and began to dress a horse in white.

***

For what might have been days, speaking to none of the other workers Ryan sullenly applied a white coat to bare wood, painted another horse while the first dried, then went back again to the first. Between each, he took long swigs from his flask.

In a corner of the room, loud enough for Ryan to hear, the foreman complained to Gideon, "Why do you always send us the hard ones?"

"And this is the easy part." Raphael's tone told of experience with these cases.

"Leave that to me," the old caretaker said.

Glaring at Nathaniel, then Raphael, then Gideon, Ryan sucked defiantly at his flask.

Gideon smiled at him and nodded. Over the next hour the whisky lost its sting and soured like milk left for days in the sun. Cursing, Ryan heaved the flask at the old caretaker. Everyone in the room faded when it slammed against the wall.

Raphael grabbed the strap of Ryan's overalls and pulled him to the corner where Nathanial and Gideon once again stood.

"This isn't working," the old caretaker said. "Only thing left is to send the boy to the wood mill shop."

"Ain't ready—"

Gideon cut Raphael off. "Don't have a choice. You know what this delay means to the others."

"He ain't seen that yet," Nathanial said.

Ryan's eyes shot fire at them. "What the hell are you talking about? I've seen—" He pushed up close to the foreman. "You don't wanna *know* what I've seen."

Gideon glanced around the noisy paint shop—at the men in overalls who laughed and poked each other as they slopped paint on a score of wooden chargers, at the bright drips on the slatted walls. "Didn't learn what he needs on the carousel," he said. "It's clear he won't learn it here, either."

"What, then?" Nathanial asked.

"The boy needs to build his own horse instead of painting over what those before him made. Yes, that's the answer." Over his shoulder, Gideon called out, "Ezekiel!"

At the mention of his name, a man, as round as a beach ball in both body and head and just as bald, stepped forward.

Ryan grunted. Without liquor to explain them, these sudden appearances were downright disturbing. And damned annoying.

"Anger seethes in this one, Zeke," Gideon said. "It's driving him on a reckless run. We have to get it released."

"Might be it's too locked in," the round man replied. "If it is, ain't nothing we can do."

"He's right," Nathanial agreed. Raphael nodded.

The caretaker pulled the wrench from his overalls and beat it against his palm. "I won't believe that. If we use it right, make his anger build enough pressure—" He glanced around. "Nick and Charlie will know what to do."

He waived the wrench like a magician's wand, and the paint shop faded into the fog. Raphael, Nathanial, Gideon, the paint crew were gone, their voices only the dim echo of memory. Ryan was now alone with Ezekiel in a gray twilight with no walls, roof, or floor.

The round man beckoned, then pointed to a closed door, which seemed to float in space. Light flickered from under the door, thunderclaps burst from behind it.

Ryan clasped the back of his head and ducked.

With a firm hand, Ezekiel lifted him from his crouch.

"Thomas, this way if you please."

His eyes flashing panic, Ryan planted his feet. *I've had enough of this! Not going a step further.*

"I'm waiting, Mr. Ryan." Ezekiel's voice was as firm as his hand.

His lips tight and his eyes narrowed, Ryan shook his head. Against his will, his feet inched forward.

"After you." Ezekiel threw the door open and stood aside with a wide grin.

"What're you laughing at?" Ryan snarled.

"The vanity of your stubbornness. Now, in here if you please. You don't have forever. Not yet."

***

Beyond the door was a vast, well lit room. Raw pine planks climbed vertically from the floor to rafters high above. At two-thirds of the room's height, stacks of lumber rested on a line of two-by-eight beams. Wires from band saws snaked upwards. Unpainted horses' heads, torsos, legs, hung from cords dropped from the roof. On the floor youngsters traced patterns onto blocks of wood, while older men—journeymen, Ryan thought they must be—roughly cut the parts at whirring machines. A platform with long tables was built out from the far wall. On it a few others, whom Ezekiel said were Master Carvers, carefully shaped each piece. On the right, a rickety staircase rose to a loft. On the left, horns blared and cymbals crashed from band organs in various stages of assembly. From those instruments came the crackle of lightning and the roll of thunder.

Barely through the door, Ezekiel braced his hands like a megaphone around his mouth, and called, "Nicholas, Charles, come here please."

At a table on the platform, Nick was rapping a wooden mallet against a chisel. A soft aura flickered around him. Laying his tools aside, he tapped Charlie's shoulder. As they trudged over, Nick grumbled, "I told ya me and Charlie hadda work. Didn't I tell ya that?"

"Sure you said it, but I thought... The three of us were together again, having fun, and—" In the slight pause, Ryan built a head of steam. "Hey, you asked me to come back, work at the factory. Heard you say that clear!"

Charlie sneered. "Not this far or this long."

Nick piled more on: "I was bein' polite. You was meant to go home and forget us once the ride ended."

"Ain't going back there. Never!" Spittle clung to Ryan's lips.

"You was always too soft," Nick said. "Never understood why the colonel put you in charge."

Ryan clenched his fists.

From the stairs to the loft, Gideon shouted, "Zeke, stop them!" He leaned over the handrail. "It's too soon for this. Can't you see inside the boy? Keeps at it now, his gears will freeze. Look, man, look. Use more than your eyes to see."

"If you say so..." His forehead creased with uncertainty, the round wood mill boss wiped his pudgy hands on the seat of his denim overalls.

Gideon rushed down the stairs, pushed the boys apart. "Not yet!" he said. Then to Nick and Charlie, "You have to finish his teaching. One step at a time. He has to build something to show at the end."

Charlie sighed.

"You were his responsibility in France. He's yours here," Gideon insisted.

"But—"

"No argument, Nick. You'll remain in this shop until he's ready, and you've been here too long." With a curt glance at the boys, the caretaker led Ezekiel away.

Nick grabbed Ryan's arm, and pulled him to the platform and up to a table that held a large block of basswood. "Watch what I'm doin'," he said as he drew the outline of a horse's rump with the stub of pencil he took from behind his ear. "See, careful. The line's gotta be just so."

Ryan tried.

"No, no!" Nick erased Ryan's hesitant marks. "Damn, gotta do everythin' myself."

"You don't." Ryan poked out his chin. "Gimme a chance, why don't you."

"Had enough of 'em already," Nick said. "Only one way to teach a blockhead."

"Nick!" Gideon's voice boomed from above.

"Yeah, yeah—"

"A little patience, please," Ezekiel said.

With a sigh, Nick pulled a wooden template from his overall pocket. "Here, use this to trace the line."

"Could've given me that before," Ryan complained as he snatched the template.

"Yeah, could have." Nick inspected the horse's leg Ryan drew. "Uh-huh. Leastwise you can do somethin' right. Now let's see ya cut it."

Ryan lugged the block to a band saw.

Nick grabbed his hands. "No, twist it like this. Look at what way the grain goes. Don't ya know nothin'?"

The band saw hummed. Though he tried to emulate his friend's motions, Ryan's first cut split the block. Feeling embarrassment rise to his face, he said, "My hand's shaking. Some whiskey would settle me. Got any hid back here?"

Cymbals from a band organ crashed. A snare drum beat a tattoo.

Nick rolled his eyes. "Useless! Hear that, Gideon? It's useless."

"That's as it may be," floated down from the loft. "If it were easy you wouldn't still be here."

Charlie sighed.

Nick ran a hand through his dark curls. Again he demonstrated the way the wood had to be cut. Ryan duplicated what he did, but again the block split. After the third time through, Nick call out, "Zeke, this ain't gonna work."

The wood mill boss stomped down the stairs. "Got to keep at it. Push him harder." He looked up to the loft, and added. "Just not all at once."

So Ryan was pushed. Under relentless prodding he rough-cut a horse's legs, then carved the body. He shaped it with a chisel and sanded it, then glued the pieces together. As the horse took form, he could almost feel it come alive in his hands.

Next came the head, the most intricate work. Concentrating, Ryan now quickly learned each new task.

Charlie hitched up the back of his pants. "Don't look so pleased with yourself. Shit, we made legs look like at a gallop the first day here."

"Usin' the wrong chisel again!" Nick spit on the floor through the space between his front teeth, then yanked the tool from Ryan's hand.

"He ain't never gonna get it right," Charlie muttered. "Damn, Nick, it's gettin' late. What're we gonna do?"

"You'll keep teaching him," Ezekiel called from the loft.

The boys did. Ryan spent an entire day smoothing his horse's skin with fine-grained sandpaper.

Nick ran his hand down the wooden neck. "Not enough yet. Not nearly enough. Do it again!"

"Ain't done till it's smooth as a baby's arse," Charlie said. "Like this! You too blind to see the difference? Maybe too drunk?"

Hanging his head, Ryan said, "I ain't drunk. Haven't had a sip since…" He screwed up his face as he tried to recall how long it had been since he'd left Paddy's Pub. "I ain't drunk," he muttered, and picked up another sheet of sandpaper.

"Got no feel for this at all. Never could do nothin' right," Nick said.

"I can!" Fire in his eyes, Ryan leaned ominously close, but quickly bit back his simmering fury. He couldn't risk losing his friends again, the way he had when the world collapsed under hailstones of fire. It had been his fault.

Thinking of the medals we'd win, what they'd write about us in the newspapers, it was me who volunteered The Musketeers to go over the top... He swallowed a sob.

"Damn idiot!" Nick said. "Why do I gotta keep showin' ya this?" He snatched the worn-out sandpaper and replaced it with another sheet. "Do it again!"

"How many times?" Ryan groaned.

"Till it's right. Till ya understand. Won't be done till then."

With a mallet and chisel, Ryan worked on his horse's face.

"Slow, smooth cuts like this." Charlie took the chisel to demonstrate.

This time Ryan did it perfectly.

Still, Nick shouted, "That's not a fierce look! It's—"

"Pitiful." Charlie wiped his nose on his sleeve. "Might as well paint tears in that horse's eyes, 'cause there ain't nothin' inside you anymore."

Organ music spiraled up until it filled the room. Ryan threw the tool at Charlie's feet. "That's it! I'm not taking any more, even from you," he yelled. "We're gonna have it out right now."

Nick laughed. "Gonna try 'im yourself, no hooch to back ya up?"

Ryan raised his fist. "Don't need nothing but this to take either of you."

From the bottom of the stairs, Ezekiel called up to the loft, "Gideon?"

The caretaker's voice carried over the din of the shop: "Ryan's finished his horse. He's ready. Let them go."

His arms at his sides, Charlie made no attempt to block the punches that crunched his ribs, shattered a tooth, and lifted him from the ground.

"Feel better now?" Nick said. He sounded weary. His face looked drained.

Ryan stepped back, staring at his clenched fists in disgust. He'd once again failed his friend. "Charlie!" This was a cry from his gut, from a year in the past. "I didn't mean—" Then the dam burst. Tears he'd held back too long doused the flames of his anger. "Why'd you make me do that?"

"Had to," Charlie said. *He* now had an aura about him. "Don't ya see, Tommy? Been so damn mad at yourself—there wasn't no other way to get it out."

Ryan's head dropped to his chest. As he ran both hands across his head and through what felt like stringy hair, a memory flickered:

"We can do it, Colonel," he heard himself say.

Now they were in a shell-rutted, mud field. Barbwire stretched in every direction. In trenches a hundred yards ahead, Hun helmets, pointed like they were topped by spears, bobbed up and down. Rifles were raised, then withdrawn to reload.

"Stay low, keep your heads down. I promised I'd get you home safe," Sergeant Tom Ryan shouted.

He and Nick and Charlie crawled across the field.

"Get your asses down!"

Barbed wire over there—get through it, they'd be near the Hun line. Drop their grenades fast, get back.

"Me first, then Nick, then you, Charlie." He slithered up, wire cutters in his hand. Snipped the wire, held it back. *"Wait for me!"* he called after them. He was tangled in the wire. *"Wait for me!"* he shouted again as Nick and Charlie crawled into the rattle of guns.

A long screech drowned out his commands. In a moment the screech dissolved into the flash of an exploding star. The world was ending. Arms covering his head, he buried his face in the mud. It felt as if it were raining.

"Nick! Charlie!"

Shrapnel splashed an inch from his head. No, not shrapnel. He lifted what had once been his friend's boot—

Ryan sniffed. "Shouldn't have said we'd go out there. I'm sorry, so…" His shoulders slumped.

Charlie stood up and brushed sawdust from his pants. "Didn't change nothin'."

Ryan moaned, "You're wrong. If I'd let us stay nested in our bunker—"

"A shell would've gotten them the next day," Ezekiel said. "See, boy, it was meant to be."

"No! It would've been different!" Ryan insisted. "Nick, I promised your ma. I swore to her—"

The round wood mill boss shook his head. "The world gone mad, that kind of promise isn't yours to make."

Ryan spun toward him, his hands balled into fists. Before he could strike, Ezekiel took his hands in a grip, which was firm, yet gentle. "The fight's over, Thomas."

Twisting his head to hide burning eyes, Ryan moaned, "Why didn't I—" With a quick motion he wiped his tears.

"Die with us?" Nick wrapped an arm around his friend's shoulders. "We know ya gladly would've. But, Tommy, ya gotta let us go."

"I… can't," Ryan said. Again he rubbed a sleeve across his eyes.

Ezekiel rested a hand on his shoulder. It felt like no more than a breeze ruffling his shirt. "You can hold them in a different way, Thomas."

"How?"

"By living. By remembering. By telling what it was like. That's what *you're* meant to do."

Tears clouded Ryan's vision. He made no attempt to wipe them away.

"Tell 'em, Tommy. Tell 'em all of it." Nick's voice seemed to come from another room.

Ryan reached again for the anger, which had kept him going. He couldn't find it.

The band organ fell silent, the saws stopped rumbling. Workmen no longer shouted to each other across the shop. When Ryan looked up, the tables, the saws, everything and everyone had vanished. It was dark. He was alone amid cobwebs and dust in the boarded-up factory.

Had he been dreaming? Absently, he reached for the flask in his overalls. "Huh?"

He was dressed in the creased jacket and trousers he'd worn when he broke into the roundhouse. *Yeah, it was nothing but a drunk dream.* He pulled the tin flask from his pocket. As he raised it to his lips, something in the empty wood mill caught his eye: near the stairs to the loft was the unpainted horse he'd built.

"It was real! All of it... happened?" He sank down with his back against the wall.

A shadow drifted down the stairs from the loft, floated closer and took form.

"It's time, Tom," Gideon said.

"For what?"

"The repair needed here is done. Nick and Charlie have moved on in their way, just as you must do in yours."

"But, I wanna stay with my friends, keep doing what they taught me."

The caretaker's ancient eyes turned down to him. His mane of white hair seemed to be blown by a wind Ryan didn't feel. "As to your work—" He pointed to the unpainted horse. "There's still a lot to be done before that's finished."

"Why?" Ryan cried.

"Why did they die that night while you came home? That's a mighty big question, son, and it isn't one I can answer in a way you'll understand."

"Why not let Nick or Charlie come home?" Ryan said. "They were—"

"Your friends." Gideon glanced toward the loft. "They loved you, son. Would either of them have wanted you to die instead?"

Ryan opened his mouth and closed it again.

"We knew you wouldn't let them go quietly. But, now that they've gone, Tom, you have to honor them."

"Don't know how."

"You do. You will," Gideon said.

"I'm a drunk is all."

"If you don't tell what happened to them, to you—what the ground looks like at the door to hell—who will?" Gideon's voice was as soothing as a lullaby. Ryan began to drift. He fought it, but was helpless to hold back the sleep overtaking him.

***

Late in the night, two police officers stomped through untamed grapevines crawling along a fence and up the trunks of tall oaks in back of the boarded-up carousel factory. Halfway through their patrol, one officer abruptly stopped. He jabbed an elbow at his partner and pointed into the shadows at the edge of the roundhouse. "Hey, Murphy, what's that?"

"Not seeing anything, Ed."

Officer Clarkson insisted, "No, over there—just at the end where the pipes touch up against the wall. I saw something move." With high steps, he waded through the weeds.

"Nothing but a pile a rags, I think," Murphy called as he followed.

When they got to the spot, the two men looked down.

"Nothing but a rag pile, huh?" Clarkson said. He kicked gently at a body curled on the ground. Blond hair, which might have been straw, was splayed around its head.

"Probably a drunk sleeping it off 'fore going home to the wife," Murphy said as he knelt to poke the body with his stick.

Clarkson prodded it with the side of his thick-soled shoe. "C'mon on, Mac, get up."

The figure stirred. Head raised, he turned his face slightly. An eye opened. "Whaaa?" It was a hoarse moan, barely human. Running his tongue along parched lips, the man slowly sat up and blinked, as if the full orange moon threw down too bright a light.

"Will you look at this," Murphy said.

Clarkson pulled off his cap and slapped it against his thigh. "Damme, if it ain't Tom Ryan. Where've you been, boy?"

"Been?" Ryan gazed around. "Down by Paddy's, having some—"

Murphy scanned the young man's face. "Down at Paddy's, is it? When?"

"Just... earlier tonight. Go ask him, why don't you." Ryan slumped against Murphy's shoulder when he tried to stand. "Can't believe I'm this stiff. What time is it?"

Clarkson dug for the pocket watch in his coat. "Two-thirty in the morning."

Ryan swatted his ear. "Must've fallen asleep here a few hours." Again he swatted.

Murphy looked the young man up and down.

"Much longer than that, I think. Boy, it's October twenty-first. Last time anyone seen you was August. Your ma raised quite a ruckus when you went off that way."

"October? That... that's impossible. I just left Paddy's." Ryan took a step back. His eyes wide, as if desperate, he looked from one face to the other. "Impossible... just been a couple of hours."

Murphy pursed his lips. "And I suppose your hair came back, and you grew that scruffy beard in just a few hours?"

As if afraid of what he might feel, Ryan moved his hand hesitantly to his chin, then to his head. "I… I wasn't dreaming," he murmured as his knees gave out.

***

The officers took the ragged young man to DeGraff's Hospital, where he stayed in a second floor ward for three days. It was a long, twenty-cot room, as white as a winter ice storm. Behind curtains, men moaned through the DT's. Nurses rushed in to inject morphine when a patient thrashed against the leather straps binding him to a steel bedframe.

Ryan needed none of this attention. His only symptom was a preternatural calm. He refused to say where he'd been, or what he'd been doing. When pressed about it, he shook his head, and said, "I gotta think this out."

Doctors and nurses, the two police officers who stopped by to ask questions, and Ryan's mother who refused to leave his bedside, said they noticed a cornered animal no longer seemed to make its home in his eyes.

Sitting on a cheap wood chair turned backward, his chin resting on it, Officer Clarkson told Ryan what had happened when he'd gone missing. Because of their argument, he said, suspicion fell on George McGuire. But, McGuire had been at Paddy's until well past two in the morning, and his wife swore she'd heard the 2:35 freight whistle up from the Central tracks when he opened their back door. Impossible he could've done anything between Paddy's and his home, police interest in him soon faded. A day was spent dredging the canal to see if a drunken misstep had toppled Ryan in. Clarkson laughed when he described what was brought up: Sludge, a couple of cracked wagon wheels, the prow of a sunken barge. Must've gone south along the tracks, looking for a good time down in Olean, the police concluded.

Now, at Ryan's bedside, his mother wept. "Doesn't matter where he's been. My boy's home."

***

The story of his missing three months wasn't told until a week later when family and friends gathered at Paddy's to celebrate Ryan's return, though at the evening's start he still refused to speak of it. That changed when the bargeman, George McGuire, strolled in just as the large clock behind the bar chimed ten.

"Glad you've come by," Ryan said to him. "I owe you an apology."

Rubbing the stubble on his chin, McGuire stared at Ryan's outstretched hand.

"Won't you take it, George? I truly am sorry to have defamed you so wrongly."

"What's brought this on?" the big man asked.

"Let's just say I learned a thing while I was... uh, away."

Everyone's eyes turned to Ryan. In the silence that followed, he came to a decision. "Paddy, pour everyone a drink—none for me," he said. Settled on a stool, he stroked the groomed version of his new beard, and glanced around. "I know this'll sound strange—crazy even. Fact is I'm having trouble believing it myself. But, there doesn't seem to be another explanation—"

With a sigh, he spoke of what he'd lost in France—the horrors he'd witnessed, and the torn and broken remnants of humanity left when Hell's door was shoved opened. Then, hesitating often, he told of what Gideon had helped him find in the Carousel Factory. This last part seemed to cause some to scratch their heads. Others nodded when he was done, their belief in a mysterious universe confirmed.

It was well past midnight when Tom Ryan finished his tale. "Now I've told it all," he said, and leaned back on his stool. He felt drained. "Hey Paddy, how's about a cuppa joe over here?" He had no need to call down the length of the bar. The bartender had been standing nearby, elbows resting on the counter.

The clatter of the coffee mug when Paddy put it down rattled like a horse's trace in the hushed room. Ryan sipped at the steaming liquid. "Yeah, I've told it all," he repeated.

In the telling, he at last understood what he was meant to do. "Can't let this happen again," he said. "Not never. Chasing after glory's a fool's quest, and mothers weeping for their sons because of it... No, it shouldn't be." Swiveling on the stool, he looked squarely at George McGuire. "So you see, I was wrong in saying you're yellow. If we'd all refused to go—" He shook his head and let the words hang. Then, cheeks puffed, he said, "World gone mad... Yeah, mad world, lusting after... what? What was it for? No, George, if we'd all stayed put—" He sat up straight. "So will you shake my hand, George, and have a drink on me?"

A look of uncertainty in his eyes, the big man gazed at Ryan.

"Held onto ill feelings got no place here," Ryan urged, his hand still outstretched. *No, got no more place here anymore than you do, Nick, or you, Charlie*, he thought.

***

The party broke up a short while later. Quietly, each who'd heard Tom Ryan's strange tale went his own way. As did the people, comments on what he'd told them went in different directions. Some, like Nick Bodoni's mother, believed it—clung to it like a life raft the rest of her days. Others said it was a drunken dream, or a story concocted to hide the fact he'd run off down the tracks to Ellicottville or Olean, stayed drunk for three months, and maybe slept with a few easy women.

In time, speculation over what happened to Ryan faded into news of greater importance. The *Tonawanda News* ran a banner headline:

ARMISTICE SIGNED.
GREAT WAR'S GUNS FALL SILENT

A hundred thousand men marched home, and with them came the artists and artisans who built the carousels at Herschell's. On a bright June morning, the boards came down from the factory's doors and windows. A fresh coat of red paint dressed its walls, and the sound of band organs could again be heard on Thompson Street.

But, the strange affair of Tom Ryan hadn't ended yet. In August of 1919 he hired on to apprentice at Herschell's. He didn't stay one long. Within weeks he demonstrated the skills required to build the great horses from start to finish. With no training he was an expert Master Carver, and many of the fierce chargers born at the Carousel Factory over the next forty years were the product of his imagination.

Herschell's is closed now, has been since 1969. In its place there's a museum to help people remember what used to be. Ryan's photograph hangs on a wall in the old wood mill shop. Dressed in denim overalls, he's sanding the wood horse that now stands behind a rope just below his picture. Tacked to its side is a sepia photograph of a young Tom and two others, dressed in old-fashioned military uniforms.

By the time he died in 1976, Ryan had told and retold the story of Gideon and the boarded-up carousel factory many times. His children and grandchildren carried the tale with them when they moved away after the Erie Barge Canal closed, and with it, half the businesses in North Tonawanda. They repeated it at sit-ins during another war.

Ryan's story has been forgotten by new generations. Still, some folks claim when the moon floats high over what used to be Herschell's factory, they hear a band organ echo in the distance. Those who hold their breath and listen say they hear the breeze whisper, "Remember."

Maggie's End

In 1804 in Osgoodshire, England, still in her teens, Maggie Forrest cringes in a small stone cell, awaiting the hangman's kiss. A clatter when the scaffold is tested in the prison yard screams in her ears. What brought her to this place? Yes, there was the trial…and what led to it.

Chapter One
Osgood Gaol

𝒞arly on a morning in July 1804, a door creaked on iron hinges inside Osgood Keep. Hurried footsteps and a few muted voices echoed in the prison courtyard. Hooves clopped along the cobblestones. A farmer's dray bumped over wood slats beneath the stone gate erected at a time beyond recall: a time of Gaels, Saxons, and Roman legions. A time of barbarity. To Maggie Forrest this was still such a time.

The slam of falling boards added a discordant note to the dawn symphony.

"Hangman's testin' his trap," someone in a nearby cell murmured.

Maggie groaned. Those words might have been a whispered herald of her fate. Skirts bunched in her lap, she cowered in a corner, and pulled at her hair that was as coarse and soiled as the week-old straw spread across the stones of her small cell. Her anxious fingers shredded the bloused sleeve of her bodice where it had been ripped when the baby was torn from her arms. Her lips formed the words, "Hail Mary, full of grace…" With the faith of the child she still was, she begged God to freeze the sun so it would never reach its zenith over the Keep. Though the prayer rose from deep within her, she did not dare utter it aloud for fear the guard might hear and denounce her as an unrepentant heretic who still, at her end, prayed for unnatural things. If Reverend Holloway were told of her prayer, he would insist she be flogged for wishing the sun would do something he preached it should not. Or maybe be burned alive instead of flogged. Old Enid Sharp had said such a punishment was still practiced when someone was accused of witchery in England.

They'd been in the kitchen of Lord Westmore's manor when the cook told her that. Was it only a year ago? With all she'd been through since—the denouncement, the trial—it was difficult for Maggie to recall. She did remember, though, how the old woman's words crackled like hens on the hearth-spit when she said, "It's a witch's punishment, burnin' is. And it ain't always in the hereafter when it's done."

This was the moral of the story Enid told after a gypsy girl was caught stealing a golden Virgin from the church.

"Cast a spell so's no one would see her do it, they say," the kitchen crone murmured. "By God's grace, the spell didn't take. Still, might be Lord Westmore will give her to the Church for to get the *old* treatment."

Though the kitchen was hot on that year-ago summer evening, Maggie had shivered. *The gypsy's no older than me,* she'd thought. Her face pinched, she'd pulled her chair away from the hearth, and drawn up her legs. "But, it… it's 1802," she'd said. "There's been no burnin's long as anyone remembers."

Flames flickering in the hearth had reflected on the walls.

Enid shook her head. "*I* remember. I weren't no more than a child the last time it were done. A witch they says that one were, blasphemin' against God."

Old eyes clouded, she'd waved her spoon as if it were a wand that might conjure up the scene. In hoarse whispers she'd recalled the pyre, the snap of burning flesh, the acrid odor. Pointing a bony finger, she'd concluded, "Hear what I say, girl. Stay a good Christian who don't never steal, fornicate, nor blaspheme. This village of Osgood Dell ain't London."

Now Enid's warning rang in Maggie's ears like the morning bell above the village church. In her dank Osgood Gaol cell, she sobbed with regret for not heeding it.

Chapter Two
The Gaoler and the Maid

Quick steps clicked in the courtyard, drew near, and stopped at the cellblock door.

"Breakfast for ye, Tom," the kitchen maid called.

The brassy voice was easy to recognize. The woman's daughter had been a friend until Maggie hid herself away in shame.

The guard, his gruff voice grating like the rusted hinges of the opening door, said, "Lor', a man could starve waiting for ye, woman."

"Och, ye think I got nothin' better to do than tend to the likes of you?"

The guard snorted. "And I got nothin' better to do but wait with this rabble till ye come." From her cell down the hall, Maggie heard his loud, long yawn. "Leastwise, there'll be one less of 'em to hear cryin' tonight."

The kitchen maid giggled. "Aye, little Maggie Forrest'll make a merry sight, doin' the gallows dance."

The swish of broadcloth skirts whispered in the hall.

She's playin' at how I'll twist on the rope, Maggie thought. Shrinking into a corner of her cell, hands at her throat, she retched a dollop of acrid bile.

The guard clapped. "That she will. Got no breakfast for 'er?"

"Food for the likes of that?" the maid said. "She don't need to meet the Devil with a full belly. I'll bring her bread and gruel home for my Hal to eat. It'll give him a stiff staff for me tonight."

With a simper in his voice, the guard replied, "If it's pleasurin' ye want, gimme the food. I'll fix you up right good."

"Pleasuring," Maggie whispered, and held her ears as if she might silence the voice of her memory. Pleasuring was what *he* had called it the first time he took her hand to show her how. After a while she had learned. Doing it right, quick, was the only way to make him stop, and put an end the searing pain that tore through her, as if her woman's part were being ripped open.

A flirtatious laugh pulled Maggie back from the past. With a light trill, the maid sang, "You askin' me to tumble in the hay with ye—me married and all?"

The guard's laughter had a leering undertone. "Married to Hal like you're married to half the men in the village. When are ye gonna give me a turn?"

"Ah, g'won with ye. It's talk like that what's gettin' little Maggie Forrest hanged this noon."

"Weren't just talk did for 'er. It were doing it, so's they say." The guard clicked his tongue. "Been me what got to 'er, would've been more than one bastard babe she bore."

Again Maggie's past danced along the gray stones of her cell. It bounced on the straw mattress of the low bed lining one wall. *There* was *more than one. The first came early, never drew a breath.* Arms wrapped around her chest, she rocked back and forth as if cradling a lifeless infant. With keening sobs, she mourned its loss now as she had then.

The guard kicked at her cell door. His bloodshot eyes peered through the barred window. Rubbing the stubble on his cheek, he sneered. "Too late for cryin'. Should've thought of that afore ye spread your legs so easy... 'Course, if you was to ask nice, I might come in, give ye one last—"

She spat at him.

His curses drew growls from the other inmates.

"Stop your complainin'," the guard snarled at them. "Ain't no hangman waitin' to kiss *your* arse goodbye."

Receding footfalls marked his march down the hall. Every few steps brought the sharp crack of his stick against a cell door.

"Two years jailed in this hole for debt, hangman'd be a welcome sight," a voice in one of the cells muttered.

The guard snickered. "If it's the hangman you'd be wantin', I can arrange that right quick. It's easier to get your head into the noose than out of it."

Maggie slouched against her cell door, her face in her hands. *They laugh at pleasuring each other and bearing babes outside the covenant. They do it for sport, and this day I'm to get the hangman's kiss, having had no choice.*

Overwhelmed, she shouted, "Stop it! Stop!" Grasping the window bars, her knuckles white, she begged, "Please. Ye don't know... none of ye know what's been done to me!"

Chapter Three
The Gamekeeper's Wife

Maggie Forrest was the daughter of Ruth, Lady Westmore's seamstress. In 1803, Amos, her father, short, gaunt, hair greased with lard from the last boar he'd slain, was the Lord's gamekeeper. They dwelt in the small stone cottage built out from the gate of Westmore Manor. It had two rooms set aside for sleeping, and a modest central space with a hearth where they did everything else. Maggie was twelve then, and comely. While other girls her age looked like children, her wide hips made her skirts sway when she strode along the village street, and lads young to old stopped to stare, their eyes fixed on her full breasts.

Walking alongside her daughter one day, Ruth saw Maggie's eyes turn to the lads, and her lips part with the slightest of smiles. She grabbed Maggie and roughly spun her around. Face taut, brown eyes glaring, she warned, "Stay far from 'em! Don't never let one catch ye alone. You're a child still, and got no need of knowin' the pain brought by what hangs twixt their legs."

Maggie twisted away, fearing if her mother looked in her eyes it would be clear she already knew.

That night, her father took his bow from a corner of their living space. "Belly's fallin' outa me for a feed of venison stew," he announced as he cracked the door open and peered out.

Next to him, pulling at her skirts, Ruth Forrest moaned, "Please, Amos, don't. What if you're caught?"

Grumbling as he always did, he shoved her aside. "Stop worryin', woman. I'll have what I want an' none's the wiser."

"Lord Westmore's law is harsh on poachers in his woods." Ruth tried to close the door. "If you're caught—"

Amos's narrow face creased. "Ain't never gonna be. Never been seen out there—'cept when I'm huntin' 'longside the lord. And then only when I let him see me."

Maggie was on a low stool by the hearth, bent over the livery trousers she mended. The fire cast an innocent glow on her face. Tilting her head, she said, "Why do you worry him so, Ma? There's lots of deer. His Lordship won't miss one buck."

"Clever child." Amos smirked. "What's one less deer?"

In two long strides he was at his daughter's side. He stroked her cheek then kissed it. Though she tried to pull from his grasp, he held her still.

"Aye, a beautiful, clever girl," he repeated, then slipped out the door.

Ruth returned to the fire, head bowed and back bent, as if she hauled a sheaf of brambles.

"He knows to have a care, Ma," Maggie said. "Why shouldn't he have what he wants when no one's hurt by it?"

"What he wants? No one hurt?" Ruth's heavy brow arched. "Stop this foolish jabberin'! Ye know nothin' of the wants of your father's belly, so be still. Look to your work—watch now, you've dropped a stitch." Snatching the trousers, she chewed off a tangled thread. When Maggie reached to take the sewing back, Ruth snarled, "Clumsy fool, I'll do it myself!"

"Let me, Ma."

"Stop your whinin'!" Ruth threw the sewing to the floor, and glared at the door. "It's worried 'bout your father's wants, y'are? Foolish child. Who but me is there to keep you from them?"

It wasn't the hearth-fire's heat that caused Maggie to break out with red welts down to her toes.

***

In the summer Ruth Forrest fell ill with what townsfolk called the black sickness. She tossed in bed for days, her body covered in pus-leaking boils. From the depths of delirium, she begged God to end her suffering. Her prayer finally answered, her shrouded body was carried to a glade just beyond the forest path. Amos had chosen this place for her burial. His eyes moist—none could decide whether it was from grief or relief—he'd insisted she be placed where he would pass her each day.

Several women of Osgood Dell were gathered by the open grave as Ruth was lowered. Shoulders hunched, they strewed petals on her.

Amos grunted; Maggie stood apart from him, wringing her hands.

Reverend Holloway's broad-brimmed hat bobbing as if to emphasize each word, he intoned, "Yea, though I walk through the valley of the shadow of death I shall fear no evil…"

As the psalm faded into the forest, Amos grabbed his daughter's hand, and yanked her to the stone cottage.

Later, some in Osgood Dell said that was the when and why of Maggie's end. Other townsfolk were sure it began when the child first grew a woman's body, and was the real suffering her mother prayed to escape. Though the truth remains buried forever with Maggie and Amos, rumors of what happened in the stone cottage spread like the black sickness when Enid Sharp, Lord Westmore's cook, whispered her suspicion in the village. That happened in late March when Maggie went up to the manor to alter the gown Lady Westmore would wear at the Easter feast.

Chapter Four
Preparing for the Feast

"Come, child," Her Ladyship scolded Maggie, "don't dawdle so. I can't be about this all day."

She glanced around her chamber, through the arched window, then at the raw beams running across the ceiling, and then at the table on which lay the miniature portrait of herself she planned to pin on her feast dress. Other women of her class had portraits of their children to adorn their clothes. For all Lady Westmore's fervent prayers in church, God had not seen fit to bless her in such a way.

Maggie fumbled with her needle. "Sorry ma'am."

After Ruth's death, the Lady had taken Maggie as her seamstress.

Lady Westmore looked away. *That filthy gamekeeper has this child,* she thought. What right had he to have one when she didn't. Forcing the thought from her mind, she tiptoed to the mirror and swiveled right then left to examine her reflection. "Those London tailors have no skill," she muttered. "They sewed this dress for weeks, and still it's too long."

"Maybe it's them shoes you're wearin'. M'lady might want to try another pair so's we can see—"

Her attention brought back to the young seamstress at her feet—the object of her envy—her anger surfaced. "You're a country wench, what do you know? Shoes are shoes, and fashion's fashion!" Stooping to lift her hem, she again muttered, "They know such things in Paris. I should have sent it there to be sewn."

Done that, I'd have twice the fixing to do, Maggie thought. She couldn't say it, though—girls of her class never dared contradict their betters or anyone else. Silently, she tacked where the hem should fall.

"Why do you move so slowly? You used to be nimble." The Lady glanced down. "It's all the clothes you have on. How could you hope to work like this?"

Maggie pulled her heavy coat tight. "Sorry, ma'am. I'm… a bit chilled these days."

"I hope you're not getting ill. We've had quite enough illness in Osgood Dell."

"Yes, ma'am." Maggie struggled to her feet.

"Well see you don't," Her Ladyship said as she slipped out of her gown. "Do try to sew the hem straight this time, won't you? And have it back to me this evening."

***

With slow steps, Maggie shuffled from the Lady's chamber, down the narrow servants' stairs, and into the kitchen at the ancient manor's north end. There she pulled a stool to the fireplace. Still wrapped in her coat, she began to sew.

"What're ye doin' in here?" the old cook demanded. Enid's short, plump body was bathed in sweat from the fire's heat. "Got no time for the likes of you. The Westmore's will be demandin' their midday meal, and it ain't near ready."

Maggie held up the gown to show her, then returned to her work.

"Oughta be sewin' that in your own house," the cook grumbled.

Outside, new-fallen snow lay like a patchwork quilt across the great lawn. Glancing through the window, Maggie shivered. "Quicker to work here than walk down to the gate and back again. Her Ladyship grows impatient, you know, waitin' for her sewin' to be done."

Enid's eyes crinkled and her lips drew down into a frown. "Are ye sure that's the whole of it? I seen ye hobblin' like an old woman from that stone house. It's the ankles swelling. Happens 'bout this time." While she stuffed a mixture of bread, nuts, and mushrooms into the cavity of a guinea hen, she asked, "Who is it, has ye full with child?"

Maggie's head snapped up.

Turning, the old cook shook a gnarled finger. "My eyes have seen a lot of this world. Do ye not think I know what's hidin' aneath that wrap of yours?"

Face crimson, Maggie stammered, "It's… winter.

"Aye, and it's cold y'are—even in front of this fire? Feelin' the cold's one of the signs." With unexpected quickness, Enid was on the girl and snatched the coat open. "I've seen your belly grow for weeks. This be your father's greatcoat you've taken to wearin' now yours don't fit."

Maggie grabbed the coat's fretting and pulled it closed. "Been eatin' too much is all."

The cook leaned back against the work table, a bawdy grin on her lined face. "Ye belly ain't full from fowl nor venison," she said. "It's sausage has ye this way." Her smile faded and her voice grew stern. "Now be about tellin' me who it is, give us another mouth to feed from this here manor. The Lord will want to know."

Maggie shivered in her coat, not sure if the cook referred to Westmore or God—to the drudges of Osgood Dell they were often the same.

Old Enid grabbed the girl's shoulders. "Tell me!"

"It weren't no one," Maggie cried.

"Ye don't get with child from no one. Lessen you're sayin' it's God's babe."

Caught between heresy and truth, Maggie clamped her jaw. She flung Lady Westmore's gown to the floor, and fled into the snow.

Through the window, Enid watched Maggie stumble and slide as she hobbled to the gate. She saw Amos stroll down the forest path just when the girl opened the stone cottage door. Maggie stepped back from him, gesticulating wildly. He seemed to stiffen. Maggie wiped her eyes and nose on the greatcoat's sleeve, then pointed to manor.

Amos turned in that direction, squinting as if he might see past the kitchen window. She leaned close, said something. Grabbing her arm, he pulled her inside.

The cook twisted away from the window. *Amos is angry, hearing as how his daughter's been ruinated*, she thought, then realized, *How could he not know, them living there alone?*

She leaned again to the window, and peered at the cottage through a pane. When the answer came to her, her mouth fell open. Her face as white as her hair, she muttered, "It were Amos Forrest, done her."

Grabbing her black cloak, Enid threw it on with a flourish, and pulled its hood over her cap. The Westmore's dinner could wait. Reverend Holloway had to be told.

***

The Reverend lived in a narrow dwelling across the courtyard from the church. While not a manor house, it was a comfortable cottage built of whitewashed daub over a wattle of woven branches set in a timber frame. Stained oak paneling lined the interior walls. He was at his dinner table in shirtsleeves and waistcoat when Enid stormed in unannounced.

"Fornication!" he spat when Enid told of her suspicion.

Tossing his napkin across his lunch pudding, as if that would keep it from melting at the mere mention of such an act, he rose and began to pace.

The old cook stood wringing her hands in the doorway.

"Fornication," Reverend Holloway repeated, and clasped long bony fingers behind his back. "Her father? You're certain?"

Enid nodded.

The Reverend gnashed his teeth, as if chewing on the evil of such a deed. His eyes hooded, he prayed aloud for guidance. At his prayer's end, instead of proclaiming *"amen"*, he took a pinch of powder from a box on the mantel, sniffed, and sneezed. "I must tell Lord Westmore," he said as much to himself as to Old Enid. "The law must deal with this."

His wide-brimmed hat was shoved low on his head as he strode down the cobbled street. His long grey hair and black coat billowed in his wake. His eyes fixed, as if locked on the Devil, he looked neither left nor right at the black and white timbered buildings he marched past.

Enid rushed after him. Now and then she stopped, gestured and whispered to a tradesman or townswoman who emerged from a shop.

That night, the sheriff and Lord Westmore's bailiff knocked on door of the stone cottage.

Chapter Five
Trial

At the June 1804 Osgoodshire Quarter Session, Maggie and Amos Forrest were called to answer a writ of incest sworn by Reverend Joshua Holloway and Miss Enid Sharp. The case was the eighth Lord Westmore was to hear that day. Others ranged from a dispute over a boundary between two farms, to the theft of dried herbs from the apothecary. Those cases held little interest to the folk of Osgood Dell. The Forrest Case was another matter. Since their arrest, gossip about the father and daughter alone in the stone cottage had passed like mutton across the counter in the village butcher shop. It had been brought home for dinner in the thatched houses lining the road from the town to the outlying farms. In strident tones, each Sunday Reverend Holloway had preached the mortal sinfulness of the act. His sermons described in detail the weakness of men, and the Hell-fire awaiting the village Jezebel.

"Amos Forrest should've known better, takin' to his own flesh like that," the village women said. The men argued the blame was Maggie's. "A young girl with a woman's body—must be she got a woman's wants," *they* said.

All agreed on one thing: the lurid truth would be revealed at the trial. Everyone in the town wanted to be at Westmore Manor when it did.

As was the rest of the village, the manor house was built of daub and wattle set into black timber. Its Great Hall, hung with tapestries depicting armor-clad Westmore ancestors brandishing broadswords before the gates of Jerusalem, was used only on feast days and four others each year. On those four days, a large mahogany desk was placed under the coat-of-arms at the hall's far end. Twelve chairs in two rows for a jury, and a thirteenth set apart for witnesses, were placed near the desk. Tables were positioned to emulate the bar at London's Westminster Assizes. Behind those tables, a gallery of wood benches was arranged in a semicircle.

Lord Westmore sat at the desk, his black robe open to reveal a frilled shirt front. Dark hair peeked from the edges of his white periwig. The Great Hall was so silent clicking teeth could be heard as the townsfolk gnawed the lunches they brought with them.

Reverend Holloway posed on a front bench where the jury could see the damning fire in his eyes.

When the first defendant was escorted through the side door, a man next to the Reverend stopped chewing his roast chicken and whispered to his wife, "There she are. Look at 'er. She done it, awright."

Maggie wore her mother's raw linen skirts with two blue petticoats beneath. Her bodice was tied in front by a single lace. Over it, she wore a dimpled wool jacket, fretted along its hem to hide the frayed edges. The jacket was tight across her breasts, but unbuttoned at the waist where her belly bulged. Her pregnancy had neared its term.

Amos was led in a moment later. As he bent to pull at a button where his knee pants caught his sock, a woman dropped her bread on the napkin spread across her lap, and sneered. "It were him!" she said. "Went to her bed, forced himself on her. Poor Ruth. Nice, she were. It's a Godsend she didn't live to see—."

"Be still!" Lord Westmore's bailiff demanded. He leaned over the desk, shuffled some papers, then announced in a stentorian tone, "If it please Milor', the next case is Amos Forrest and his daughter Margaret. They are accused of forn—"

"Yes, yes," Westmore interrupted. He glanced at Maggie who had frozen in mid-stride, her face ashen. "I'm familiar with the allegation," he softly added.

Her eyes lowered, Maggie thanked His Lordship with a fleeting smile. Slowly, hobbling from side-to-side she reached a seat behind one of the tables. A chair leg scraped the floor and a screech of wood filled the Great Hall as she struggled onto it.

Westmore winced at the sound. Men in the village knew his wife would be in an unpleasant mood when she saw the gash the chair had left. They also knew it was Her Ladyship's moods which frequently drove Westmore to his mistress's bed, or to hunt in the forest.

As if at the pleasant thought of a deer hunt, the Lord turned his eyes to his gamekeeper, and said, "Amos, please sit here beside the jury."

Forrest grunted, and muttered an incoherent reply.

After a moment spent turning pages, Westmore glanced at him. "Now, Amos, tell us how your daughter came to be, uh… in her present condition."

"*I* could tell you what got her that way," someone in the back called out.

"Ain't but one thing done that," somebody else said.

The gallery roared with laughter.

Maggie blushed.

Reverend Holloway glared at the townsfolk, as if to memorize the faces of those parishioners who made light of this sin. A few men shrank down on the benches, fearing the Reverend would call them to task in his next sermon.

"Silence!" the bailiff bellowed.

"Thank you," Westmore said. His eyes on the Reverend, he instructed the jury, "This is a serious matter. I expect it will be treated with appropriate decorum."

Someone laughed. "Aye, decorum. Old Amos gettin' his decorum inside her's what done it, sure enough."

"You, Thomas Melrose! Show respect for this honorable court!" the bailiff shouted.

"We're waiting for your answer," Westmore said when the gallery quieted.

After a quick glance at Reverend Holloway, Forrest looked down at his hands. "Uh... I, uh... I ain't rightly sure, Milor'." He shifted on the hard wooden chair. "It weren't nothin' happened under *my* roof."

"Do you know who the father is?" Westmore asked.

Forrest's gaunt face grew as red as the bandanna around his neck. "No, sir, I don't, sir. Near as I can figure, must be some lad my Maggie took up with... Maybe more'n one for all's I know."

Tears glistened in the girl's eyes. *How can he swear that, tell 'em I'm naught but a... a common whore?*

"Now that's likely, ain't it?" Forrest rushed on before another question could be asked. "Or maybe it were someone come through Osgood Dell and left again." He turned to the jury. "That's possible."

"Unlikely, I think," Westmore said. "You know what you're accused of. Remember, Amos, you've sworn to tell the truth. Do you deny it was you?"

"Me? Milor'..." Forrest sputtered, his face now a deeper crimson. "Never! How could anyone say— Treated that girl good, I did. Fed her, give her my Ruth's clothes when she died. And how does the whelp repay me for my kindness? By sneakin' out and gettin' with child off some passin' tinker, is how."

"You live in the house with her. Surely you know of her comings and goings."

"How's a man to know what his child's about?" Forrest whined. "Can't be done I tell ye—not when I'm off in the forest, seein' after Milor's game day and night. And she's up here at the manor all the time..." He turned to the judge's desk with a smirk which suggested, *Maybe it were you, done it to her, Milor'.*

The deep frown on Westmore's face said, *This is too much!* He glared at his gamekeeper. "So you deny it was you? Having sworn on the Bible, you still say that?"

Forrest jumped to his feet with his right hand over his heart and the left one in the air. "Weren't me, Milor', I swear it!"

Maggie's emotions—fear, anger, hurt—crashed like waves against a rocky shore. Her brown eyes overflowed. *Aye, you'd swear anythin'—be the one to light the fire on me, if it'd save your scraggy skin.*

"We'll soon see about this," Westmore said. "Reverend Holloway, you're one of two who swore this writ. Please take the chair. Tell the court what you know."

Under questioning, the Reverend admitted he personally knew little against the defendants, except that neither had attended his church since Ruth Forrest passed. "But, I know what's been told to me," he said, and pointed at Maggie. "A young girl with no mother, a father with no wife— I asked God to tell me if it wasn't her who seduced *him*."

His face buried in his hands, Westmore almost laughed when he asked, "What did God tell you?"

Holloway twisted in his chair and stared at the jury. With ecumenical grimness, he announced, "God didn't deny it."

The old cook was called next. She shuffled to the witness chair wrapped in a black shawl. The long skirts tied over her chemise dusted the floor. She told Westmore she knew nothing for certain—except the girl was heavy with child. With no need to be prodded by questions, she spoke of what she saw through the kitchen window. When asked whether Maggie idled about with young men, she swore the girl was always either at home, or with Lady Westmore at the manor.

"And if she wasn't, she were off sewin' somewhere," Enid testified. "What with all the work she done for Her Ladyship, and then goin' down to clean the stone cottage, and see to that filthy Amos's wants, it's a miracle the poor child had time for laying with anyone. First off I thought it was all that work, left her quiet after the fever took her ma. But, knowin' what I know, I say it couldn't be naught but Amos Forrest poking at her, put the babe in her belly."

The townswomen smiled smugly when Enid finished. The men snorted and sneered.

Now it was Maggie's turn. Struggling from her seat behind the table, she lurched toward the witness chair. When she was settled, Lord Westmore said to her, "Child, you've been with a man, there's no denying it. The only questions are who it was, and did you go with him willingly."

She buried her head in her hands. *Was I willin'?* She thought. *Not the first times he come to me in the night whilst Ma slept. But the nights after that and all those times day and night since she passed? Pleasure me, Maggie, he told me. Your Ma don't care to no more. It weren't no pleasure for me, though. Not whilst I tried to fight him off me.* When she realized she couldn't, she had lain quiet and let him do what he would. It was then her body, with a mind of its own, grew aroused—though she willed it not to—and great swells of pleasure coursed through her. She hated it. Hated him. She hated herself and her body for the way it reacted. Yet, having felt the pleasure once—

"Come, Maggie, tell us who did this to you," Westmore said in the hushed hall.

Her teeth clenched, she shook her head.

"You must say his name. There's no crime if it were a village lad, and you were willing."

Her heart aching, she glanced at the townsfolk in the gallery. These were people she'd known all her life. Condemnation seemed to burn in some eyes. The moist glitter of pity filled others.

"Say his name, girl!" a woman shouted.

"Silence!" the bailiff shouted back.

Maggie looked at the twelve men who would decide her fate. They glanced away.

"And you've no part in this crime if it were done to you, but you weren't willing," Westmore prodded.

"Say who it were," the gallery murmured.

Done to me, she thought. The shame and grief she'd locked inside steamed like water sprinkled on hot coals. *Of course it were done to me*. The thought caused a fire to flare. With a whooping sob she stood and pointed to Amos. "It were him! He done this! He hurt me. Didn't want him, but he—" She sank back in the witness chair, and tore at her jacket sleeve as the fullness of the crime burst from her. "Oh, God, he's my Pa!" she cried, and tumbled to the floor with her flaxen hair pulled over her face.

A collective gasp rose from the gallery.

Amos sprang up, looking to the jury. "It weren't me! For pity's sake, you men know me."

Westmore glared at him.

"It weren't me, Milor'!" He pointed at his daughter. "It were her! She's a witch. Cast a spell. The slut *made* me do it."

What might have been a satisfied smile crossed Reverend Holloway's lips. The gallery erupted, everyone chattering at once. The bailiff's command failed to silence them.

Westmore stood and rapped his gavel. "Stop this at once! I'll have you all removed!"

When order was finally restored and the bailiff had helped Maggie back to her seat behind the table, Lord Westmore called Amos back to the chair. "Well, Forrest, what do you have to say for yourself?"

His face as white as the walls of the Great Hall, Amos twisted to face the jury. "It were her what climbed into *my* bed," he moaned. "Told her not to, but—" He shrugged. His eyes seemed to ask, *Wouldn't you also be seduced by a child who looks like this?*

Murmurs again swept through the gallery. Westmore rapped his gavel. "You just swore before this court it was not you who has Maggie with child."

Forrest looked miserable. "I… I did, Milor'."

"Then you lied."

"No, Milor'. Well…" he glanced left, right. "I did, Milor'," he said at last. "But, it were only to protect my child. Promised my poor dead wife I'd protect her. Swore it on her grave, I did," Slouching back, he added with defiance, "An oath on a dead wife's grave is greater than any sworn on a book."

Maggie half-rose. "Aye, and who was there to protect me from you?" The words took what little strength she had left. She dropped into her chair with her head on the table.

Chapter Six
The Verdict

The jurymen turned to each other and whispered. Reverend Holloway glared at them. The bailiff rapped the gavel.

Westmore said, "You, the jury, have heard all that's to be said on this matter. It has been established that Amos Forrest is the father of the baby his daughter will bear. Now you must decide the circumstances surrounding its conception. Did the defendant, Amos Forrest, take her, or did the defendant, Maggie Forrest, lure him into the act? A crime against the peace has been committed in Osgood Dell, a felony. You must determine whose crime it is. Whilst you do, bear in mind the seriousness of the offense and the punishment awaiting the guilty." He looked then at Reverend Holloway, and added, "An example must be made so such a thing is never again done in this village."

It took the jury less than fifteen minutes to agree on a verdict. While they huddled the gallery rose and wandered about. The manor's Great Hall was alive with gestures and shouts, each person excitedly arguing the whats and wherefores of Maggie's testimony, of Amos's. A sudden silence fell over the gallery when the jury foreman rose.

Somebody whispered, "Look at their faces. That one's smiling. Must be they decided it were—"

Another cut him off. "No. That one there's somber-like. Gotta be—"

A single rap from the gavel brought everyone back to the benches. The foreman whispered to the bailiff, who turned and whispered in the judge's ear. Westmore frowned. He seemed unable to look at the jury as he asked, "Have you decided a verdict?"

Staring straight ahead, the foreman answered, "We have, Milor'."

"And what is it?"

"It were Maggie Forrest—"

The rest of what the foreman might have said was lost when the gallery's benches scraped on the floor, and men and women jumped up shouting at each other.

The bailiff shouted, "Silence!" His command unheeded, he grabbed the gavel from Westmore's hand. The desk rattled as he pounded on it.

With a deep sigh—of satisfaction or concern, Maggie couldn't tell—Lord Westmore turned to the foreman. "You're sure?"

"Aye, Milor'. We are."

He looked into the eyes of one then another of the jurors. "You all agree?"

Some nods were more eager, but all said yes.

"And you recognize the punishment the law says I must impose."

The jurors glanced at each other.

Westmore leaned back in his seat with his eyes settled on Reverend Holloway. "The law's the law, and a jury of twelve men good and true has rendered its verdict. Margaret, daughter of Amos and Ruth Forrest, you have been found guilty of instigating and carrying on incestuous relations with your father. It is the sad duty of this court to have you taken from this place, and brought to—"

Again the gallery erupted.

Maggie fainted.

Chapter Seven
Justice Rendered

That afternoon, the prison guard shoved Maggie Forrest into a dark cell at the far end of the hall in Osgood Gaol. Scratching the rough stubble on his cheek, he leered though the barred window. His voice barely audible, he said, "You're mine now—least till the hangman gets ye. Oughta be nice to me."

Maggie's breath caught in her throat, and she cowered on the straw in a corner as far from him as the small stone cell allowed.

His face breaking into a snide grin, the guard turned and began a slow march back to his post.

"Ain't naught but a swine," a voice in a cell down the hall hissed.

Maggie heard a quick step, then the sharp crack of a stick against a door. The man's fingers must have been on the bars, because the crack was followed by a yelp.

Through a mucus laugh, the guard called out, "Anyone else want a taste of me stick?"

The only response was the rustle of feet on straw as the prisoners moved back from their cell doors.

An hour later, just when the kitchen maid brought the guard his supper, Maggie howled.

"Shut your mouth!" The guard smacked his stick on the table. "Don't want me to come down there."

Now Maggie screamed.

His chair clattering, the guard stormed down the hall. Grabbing the bars on the door, he shouted, "I told ye—"

The maid caught up with him. A glance into the cell must have told her what was happening. "Ye bloody fool, Tom," she said to the guard. "Do ye know nothin'? It's her babe comin'.

"Her—"

"Don't gape there like an idiot. Fetch the midwife and be quick about it!"

Twenty minutes later, out of breath the guard returned with a bony woman in tow. The woman's family had provided midwives to the village of Osgood Dell for generations beyond recall.

The guard yanked nervously at his sweat-stained red uniform jacket. As if fearful of entering Maggie's cell, from just outside the open door he pointed. "In there."

Tsking, the midwife said, "Could ye not find a filthier hole for birthin'?"

The kitchen maid had made a nest of the straw in the cell. With Maggie's head on her lap, she used her skirts to wipe tears and sweat from the young woman's face. Glancing up, above another howl the maid said, "Done what I could. But, it's a hard one. The babe don't wanna come."

With the command, "Fetch clean water!" the midwife shoved the guard from the cell door. She knelt beside Maggie and the maid. "I'm here with ye, child?" she crooned. "It'll be all right now." She took some herbs from her bag and put them in the girl's mouth, softly saying, "Chew this." Then she pulled out a clean rag. "Bitin' on this'll help some."

Amid muted screams and howls, the hours passed. Then, in the heart of the night, Maggie's cries mixed into those of an infant. Leaning from the cell, her hair, blouse and skirts as limp as if she had been the one to give birth, in a hoarse voice the maid called to the guard, "The babe's a girl."

"Aye," the midwife whispered. "But, what'll be done with this wee whelp?" She glanced at the kitchen maid.

"She's mine!" Maggie groaned with what little strength she had. "None'll take *this* one from me." She tore the buttons from her dimpled jacket, and wrapped her newborn in it. Clutching the infant to her breast, she rolled toward the wall.

"Hush, child," the midwife said. "Ye must think of your child. What's to become of her when ye meet God?"

The kitchen maid slowly shook her head. "Don't be none'll take this bastard babe, born as it were." After thinking a moment, she said, "Amos. He sired this one—it's him'll have to take her."

Still clutching her baby, Maggie crawled back against the stone wall. "Never!" Her eyes wild, she cried, "He'll not do to her what he done to me. I'll kill my babe first." She wrapped her jacket around her daughter's face.

Still on her knees by the cell door, the kitchen maid called, "Tom, we're needin' ye!"

The guard lumbered down the hall. In a minute, he wrenched the baby from Maggie's arms.

When they left the cell and the door was locked behind them, Maggie lay whimpering in the straw.

In the afternoon, the midwife left the baby with Amos at the stone cottage. Instead of walking directly there, she had taken a path through the woods. Empathy made her do this: the child she carried in the basket over her arm would have a difficult life. Amos Forrest had not been convicted, yet his guilt was as great as his daughter's. Maybe greater. He would be shunned by the village, she knew, as would a child born of incest. It would be a mercy to leave the baby in the forest for God to do with as He would. Perhaps she ought to place the basket in the stream like Reverend Holloway preached had been done to cleanse Moses of his sin—though she couldn't conceive of a sin such an infant might have committed. For an hour, she perched on a rock at the bank of the stream with her feet dangling in the cool water, pondering this. As the sun rose high overhead, she sighed. To abandon a baby to animals in the woods would itself be a sin—a barbarity no one had considered doing since the days of the Picts and Celts.

Chapter Eight
Punishment

The Sunday prior to the scheduled execution, Reverend Holloway preached a sin so mortal could only be cleansed in the flames of Hell. It was a pity, he said, the law no longer permitted punishment at the stake. He then railed against the circulating rumor that, loath to train a new seamstress, Lady Westmore had convinced her husband to pardon the offender.

When the day arrived, Maggie Forrest was not hanged for the crime of which she'd been convicted. This was because a fire flared in Osgood Gaol just before the cart arrived to carry her through the gathered villagers to the gallows.

That morning, the kitchen maid had brought the guard's breakfast. He'd flirted with her.

"You askin' me to tumble in the hay with ye—me married and all?" she'd responded with a welcoming trill.

"Married to Hal like you're married to half the men in the village," the guard had said. "When are ye gonna give me a tumble?"

While Maggie cowered in her cell praying for salvation, the kitchen maid at last gave the guard his tumble. His trousers down, her skirts raised, in a room lit by the glow of a lantern at the rear of the prison hall, they gyrated on the floor. At the peak of his climax, the guard's arm flew out. It knocked against the table with such force the lantern flew across the room and shattered in a corner. Oil from the broken light seeped onto the dry hay, and the fire spread so quickly it blocked the door. Along with the guard and the kitchen maid, seven prisoners died in the flames. Burning embers from the wood roof of the building floated in the air and settled on shops and cottages surrounding the Keep. Townsfolk who had come to the courtyard to witness Reverend Holloway usher the condemned girl up the gallows steps and into the hereafter, rushed for water buckets. It wasn't enough. Half the village was eventually consumed.

As the Reverend walked through the gate of the Keep, with the gaol ablaze behind him he was heard to say God had rendered His own verdict. He did not offer a prayer for Maggie's infant daughter, who was now alone with Amos Forrest in the stone cottage.

***

In the following years, a rumor spread in Osgood Dell. It was said not long after Maggie's end, Lady Westmore, with her husband's bailiff in tow, went to the stone cottage. There the bailiff offered Amos Forrest a choice: he would either surrender Maggie's baby to Her Ladyship, or by nightfall his head would adorn a pike. The next day Lady Westmore left the village. The rumor said she returned to London, raised the child as her own, and lived to see her wed to a peer of the realm. Whether this was more than idle gossip, no one could say. The villagers knew only that the baby disappeared shortly after the fire at the gaol, and lady Westmore left Osgood Dell because, she told Enid Sharp, country life no longer suited her.

Thieves Game

Golf is an honorable game; on the course players don't take what isn't theirs. Does this principle apply off the course?

Half a dozen fans clicked slowly overhead. Ornamental spittoons dotted the wood floor. A player piano jutted from the wall near a staircase leading to a balustrade balcony. The only thing missing from this scene was a line of rough-looking cowhands bellied up against the bar. The ersatz western-movie bar, part of the clubhouse, was dim after a bright afternoon on the desert golf course. Men and women in shorts perched on a row of stools or slouched at the few tables, reliving the day's glory over tall, cool ones.

"Should've seen my fairway metal on fifteen," someone said. "Hit it right on the screws—cleared the lake by ten yards."

His buddy laughed. "Uh-huh, after your first two shots splashed right in the middle of the lake."

"Didn't either."

"Come on. I saw the ripples..."

Laughter rose at another table. "—told the boss my kid got sick, stole me an afternoon."

"Me too. The wife thinks I'm in Tucson with a client"

Glasses clinked throughout the room.

Where the bar curved around to swinging doors, Emil Hopkins glanced at a CNN talking head on the 52" screen hanging on the wall. He rubbed his chin while he read the scrolling headlines:

REQUIREMENT FOR PASSPORTS AT THE CANADIAN BORDER DELAYED UNTIL JUNE; PASSPORT OFFICE SWAMPED WITH APPLICATIONS; ARIZONA ILLEGAL ALIEN LEGISLATION PASSED...

When the news dissolved into a commercial break, Hopkins settled back on his stool and pulled the brim of his Stetson down until the shadow hid his eyes. Though it was actually the kind of hat his favorite golfer, Greg Norman, wore, to him it was a Stetson. After posing this way a minute, to the man next to him, he said, "If I count right partner, you owe me thirty dollars."

"Sure 'bout that?" Slade McGill responded.

Skin like tanned leather, face chiseled like a desert mesa, this man was what Hopkins would have liked to be. McGill had been born on a ranch on the free range out past Yuma during the dust storms of '32. He knew how to ride, rope, and brand calves. It was rumored in the old days he wasn't particular about whose calves they were, but McGill was tough enough to make sure his mark remained on the animals' hides.

"I'm... certain," Hopkins said, not sounding as though he were.

"How do ya figure?"

Assaulted by harshness in the other man's tone, Hopkins drew back, and began to count on his fingers. "I, uh, birdied the fifth hole. And, uh..."

McGill rested his visor on the bar next to an ashtray. From his pocket, he pulled a pouch of tobacco and some rolling papers. Leaning close with only a hint of smile, he said, "Yeah, but I got that one back—eighth hole when I parred over your bogie."

"But..." Small beads of sweat dotted Hopkins' upper lip.

McGill's laugh was so deep it might have started at his toes. "Don't fret on it, A-mill. You got it figured right." He tilted on his stool, pulled three tens from his wallet, and dropped them on the bar.

Though he laughed, McGill looked far from pleased. He rarely lost at golf, at business... at anything. Leaning across Hopkins, he bellowed down the bar, "Hey Chief, what you doing back there?" He glanced at his golfing partner with a sly grin. "Must be getting ready to raid a wagon train."

***

At the far end of the room the bartender folded his newspaper, straightened his tropical print shirt, and slowly moved down the bar. The tag on his pocket said he was Harold Coolwater. Wiry, with black hair and a bent nose, his skin color was as deep as McGill's. He wasn't a chief—not near old enough to be a tribal elder—but he was a full-blood Navajo like most of the staff keeping this small piece of desert green enough to be their wealthy patrons' playground.

"What can I get you gents?" He picked up a towel and wiped his hands.

"Couple of screwdrivers for me and my buddy," McGill said. He slapped Hopkins' back. "Use the top-shelf vodka. This eastern carpetbagger cleaned me out good today. Drinks are on him, Chief."

It was degrading to be called Chief in the tone McGill used, though far better than some things Coolwater had heard from *belegana* like these. He'd learned to ignore the curses: cross words led to fights, loss of another job. Good tips were the result of an easy, relaxed smile. Not much of a contest between the two.

"So, you took this old cattle rustler, did you?" he said to Hopkins. In five years behind the club's bar he'd learned his regulars, how far he could go with them.

"Cattle rustler?" McGill laughed and shook his head the way he might have if he'd been cussed at by a child. "Talk like that, my granddaddy would've plugged you full of so many holes, you'd have water leaking outta your hide."

Only if your granddaddy and his free-ranging friends left my granddaddy any of our water to drink, Coolwater thought. Smiling, he reached for a bottle of Grey Goose on one of the glass shelves.

Something on the television seemed to catch Hopkins' attention. "Hey, Chief, make that louder," he said.

Coolwater slid the remote down the polished bar.

The talking head was saying, "—*meanwhile, in San Diego a group of Mexican activists interrupted a school board meeting to demand that courses be taught by Spanish-speaking teachers—*"

The picture switched to a long-haired blond who looked more like a movie star than a reporter. "*That's right, Dan,*" she shouted into her microphone. "*As you can see—*" the rest was lost in the angry voices behind her.

Hopkins shook his head. "Seems to me, if people want to live here they ought to speak American."

"Damn Mexicalis," McGill snorted. "Stealing our jobs while our tax dollars dress and feed 'em."

Pushing back his hat, Hopkins said, "You've got that right."

"Speak English, dammit!" McGill hollered at the television, his tanned face now a deep crimson. Without taking his eyes from the screen, he shouted, "Hey, Chief, you a damn lazy Mexicali? Get another round down here."

"Don't know what this country's coming to," Hopkins said. "Had that at my factory, too—back in Maine that was—except they were Haitian girls, not Mexicans. But, it was the same thing. Twelve hours a day, I never knew what they were saying. Could've been putting hexes on me for all I knew. Me, who gave them jobs."

"They know better than to pull any of that around here," McGill said. "They do, we know how to take care of 'em. Spouting that heathen lingo 'stead of good American."

Because Coolwater's back was turned, neither Hopkins nor McGill saw fire flash in his eyes as he reached again for the vodka. In 1880 missionaries arrived on the

Reservation. His grandfather was a child then. Taken from his family and put into a boarding school which was more like an orphanage, he was forced to dress like the whites, talk their guttural words. When he refused, he was locked in a cellar. *Speak English?* Coolwater thought. *Got no choice. Our language of the* dinae *is almost lost. Be totally gone soon, along with our stories, songs—all we are.*

"They should build a wall, keep them out! What's wrong with the government, they can't get that done?" Hopkins shouted at the television. His voice was a higher, misshapen echo of McGill's outrage.

"Damn right," McGill said. "A-mill, my granddaddy settled this land. Wasn't nothing but sedge grass and savages here back then. Now those damn Mexicalis wanna come where they don't belong? A wall's the thing. Keep them out. Hey, Chief, what do you think about them damn foreigners with their lingo no one understands coming where they don't belong?"

A glass in one hand, Coolwater bent to pull a new container of orange juice from the refrigerator beneath the bar. He spit into the glass then filled it with juice.

"Tell me, Chief!" McGill insisted. "What do you think about that?

Coolwater straightened up, and topped the glass with a shot of Grey Goose. What he was about to do was wrong, he knew. He ought to make an excuse about the juice being sour, spill the drink into the sink and mix a new one.

"Well, I'm waiting," McGill said.

A smile on his lips, Coolwater handed the drink across the bar. "I ain't got no opinion 'bout that kind of thing. You know that, Mr. McGill."

Witches Gumbo

Superstition flows in the marshes of Bayou LaFit. A gumbo of good luck, bad fortune, and *cunjas*—hexes—fill Maudie Remillard's world. Maudie knows the old ways. Real or the stuff of imagination and suggestion, the result is the same for Luc Saleau and Pascal Remillard when they mistreat her.

Onion, pepper, celery; slice, dice, the trinity...
(A chant to teach a child to cook)

Chapter One
Maudie and Marie

Marie needed to instruct her daughter in the ways of a Cajun wife. Both would suffer if the child didn't learn. "Where's the okra? They don't be no gumbo worth setting down to if they ain't no okra in it," she scolded the moon-eyed girl.

Outside the kitchen window a heron swooped low over Bayou LaFit, dove, and soared off with a catfish. Maudie winced, feeling as though the bird's sharp beak had clamped tight on her belly. *I'm that fish*, she thought.

The weathered wood house with creaking floors had stood near the bank of the swamp more than fifty years, and little had been done to keep it in repair.

"Look at me. You gotta be listening," Marie hissed. Not much more than a sharp whisper, still the sound carried on the humid swamp air. With a shudder, she glanced out to where her husband slumped in a wicker chair, an old ceramic jug at his feet.

Maudie followed her mother's eyes. "Wake him or not, be just the same thing," she said, and turned her back. It hurt to see Marie's bruised wrists and the remnant of a blow beneath her right eye. "Why's he always do that to you?"

"Do what?"

The child touched Marie's black eye. Her voice quivering, she said, "It's 'cause of me."

Marie took her daughter's face, brushed aside her lank, stringy, brown hair, and looked into her eyes. "No, child. *Votre pere* didn't do that. I... fell. Out by the dock..."

It was a lie, same as always. Brushing at a tear, Maudie thought, *One day me and* mamere *gonna leave this place and that old drunken man.* She turned toward the window. *Someday...* They'd have to run fast and far. Maybe all the way up the Mississippi to St. Louis. *See the World Fair, ride the Ferris Wheel. That old man won't never find us on top of it.*

Dreams of escape ended when the child was thirteen. That's when Marie piled rocks in her apron, and waded through duckweed into Bayou LaFit rather than spend another moment in the house of Luc Saleau.

***

Everyone knew how Saleau treated Marie.

He was a big brooding man with thick arms and a belly grown large from beer, whiskey, and doing as he damn-well pleased. Marie was a delicate thing in body and face. Her instinct was always to please. Still he'd trip her with a mop and laugh at her for being a clumsy slob. He'd smack her with it, too, in front of friends when she didn't bring his beer right quick after he called for it. Or for any of a hundred other reasons. And he beat her with that mop when his daughter was asleep and no one else was around. Nights at the saloon he'd lift a beer, and tell in detail how her face twisted when he grabbed her arm and dragged her out for a dunking in the swamp.

"Just something to do," he'd say, belching back the bottle dregs.

Sly grins would break across the faces of others bellied up against the raw wood bar when he said that. They knew it was Saleau's way of explaining how to tame a bayou wife. No one corrected him. Most treated their wives the same way.

Fragile after so many years, one morning Marie left the house after a sleepless night. Eyes red with fever, body wrapped in a long shawl to hide the shame of one more beating, she stumbled across the lawn out back. That afternoon Maudie found her afloat like a broken cypress limb in the bayou, her face puckered and white.

"*Mamere!*" she screamed, and waded into the murky water. "No! No! Oh, *mamere*. Why'd you do this? We could have…"

She dragged the body onto the bank and knelt over it. Drenched, shivering though the sun was high and it was past ninety degrees, she cradled her mother and caressed the still face. Eyes raised to the sky, she moaned, "Come back, *mamere*. We can go from this place, just you and me."

Her keening pulled Luc Saleau from a moonshine slumber. He stumbled to the bank and shoved Maudie aside. With a grunt, he grabbed his wife's wrist and dragged her limp body to his house.

Left alone, Maudie walked two miles on the rutted road into town, her steps measured by tears. She had to beg a prayer from Pere Bonifay. It was all she could think to do.

Though he knew better, in pity for a lost soul the priest called the death an accident, and that's how Sheriff Granbeede wrote it up. But, Bayou LaFit was a small place—just a dozen or two shacks pressed against the swamp, one general store, a clinic behind the doctor's house, and a saloon up by the Five Corners where three roads crossed and Route 1 turned east toward Lafayette. In Bayou LaFit rumors simmered like swamp critters in every gumbo pot. Neither pity nor a sheriff's report could hide the true cause of death.

When word of it reached a dot of land deep in the bayou, Marie's Aunt Lillian Gaspard feared she might be to blame as much as Saleau. Most around Bayou LaFit called Lillian the Swamp Witch. A stooped, grey hag—a *vielle*— she was a hermit who lived among possums, raccoons, and gators, in a shack hidden by Spanish moss dripping from the cypress branches and chinaball trees on Snake Island.

She'd taught Marie some of the old ways for protection against Saleau's moods. It clearly wasn't enough.

Chapter Two
Marie's Gumbo Pot

While she lived, Marie Saleau was the best cook in the parish, recipes passed down through her family's generations from the first who settled in the bayou. Yet, Luc Saleau complained to Dr. Billiot, "I'm sickly 'cause that cow's too stupid to know the difference 'tween real food, and the devil weed that Swamp Witch grows. No man dare to teaching her manners, show her what's what." Luc leaned forward, struggling for breath.

"That Swamp Witch ain't no better than a mean *babette*. Make me sick with them things she tell my Marie to put in her pot. That *vielle* Gaspard," he sputtered, and fell back against his pillow. "Makes all my luck bad. Now she's trying to witch the life outta me."

Dressed in a mismatched skirt and blouse, Marie slouched against the bedroom door. Bruised from her husband's latest displeasure, she prayed for a hen to crow as a sign death nested in the crumpled sheet on his bed.

The doctor unwrapped his wire-frame glasses from his ears, and rubbed a finger across the vein running down his long nose.

"Now, Luc, you don't be believing such things?" He shook his head. In seventy years he'd heard all of Bayou LaFit's superstitions. "Isn't no potions from that harmless hermit ailing you. Just too much drinking last night, I think."

The smile creasing Marie's face was as cold as the chills wracking her husband's body.

Saleau's drinking was only part of what ailed him. The rest was indeed the combination of herbs and vegetables the Witch Gaspard had given Marie to put into her gumbo pot.

Use these onions and greens, it'll be just fine, Aunt Lillian had said in a voice as old as the craft she practiced.

This spice, too. Pour in some of that beer he likes so much, then light these blue candles. Stew it all a long time whilst you say, 'Gumbo bring me peace.' That will make Luc Saleau behave.

The spell was intended to scare Saleau. But, what wasn't calculated into Aunt Lillian's recipe was the mixture of cruelty and stupidity flowing in the man's blood. Once the spell ran its course, it was as if his illness never was. And as spells often do, this one had an unforeseen effect. While Saleau shivered for a week in bed, Marie experienced the peace denied her in a seedy hovel with a cruel slob—a *couyon*—like her husband. Having known even such a short respite, life was unbearable when it ended.

As soon as he was strong enough to roll from his piss-stained mattress, the beatings began again and were more frequent. If his traps were empty, if he twisted an ankle in a rut, or a friend's bullet sped just wide of him while they shot at 'coons during a drunken midnight hunt, he was convinced his wife had fixed a *cunja* on him, a bayou hex. He beat her with his fists to make it stop.

Cringing in a corner near her stove, she finally understood nothing she ever put into her gumbo pot would make this end.

After that, those times Marie slouched like a kicked cat into the general store, her right eye blackened and her jaw swollen, townswomen gathered round a barrel in the corner. "Saleau beat her for being a witch," they whispered, though they knew it was the last thing a sane person would do to a wife truly capable of such a craft. So, "Just chasing excuses for beating on her," they concluded. And when she drowned, they said. "Hope Maudie will be stronger than her ma." Then they looked quickly away, because in Bayou LaFit such simple prayers had a habit of becoming fact.

Chapter Three
Funerary Rite

There was no undertaker in town or anywhere around for fifty miles, so Luc Saleau dug Marie's grave. That was on a Friday—Good Friday. The same day she floated to shore at Maudie's feet. Though Bayou LaFit's dead weren't supposed to be buried on a holy day, Saleau told folks he couldn't wait because the corpse was already ripe from the heat. He wouldn't dare tell anyone the rest: that when he lifted the spade from the grave he'd dug there was blood on it, and peering into the pit he saw a red puddle glistening at the bottom. He didn't stop to think what he saw might just be clay. Superstition is stronger than logic to a man who hasn't much of the latter in stock, so to Luc it was blood, an evil sign: the mark of a *cunja*. The town would shun him if it knew, as would his drinking friends down at the saloon, fearful the hex would reach out for them.

When he saw the blood, he threw the shovel at his sheet-shrouded wife. He tried to turn and run, but was drawn back to look again into the pit. Lost in a red haze, he didn't hear his barefoot daughter come up behind.

Maudie glared at his ashen face. Her lips tight, she bent her eyes to the grave in which her *defant mamere*— mother of sainted memory—would soon lay. "You drove her to the swamp so's you could have that widow slut," she hissed, and pointed. "See that down there? It's blood. It'll make sure you don't never know a minute of peace in your life for what you done to *mamere*." *And if the cunja don't, I will*, she thought. Then drawing out the words, she said, "Gonna tell everyone what you done."

Saleau's breath caught in his throat. How could Maudie know of his affair with the widow from over by Route 1? He'd been quiet about it, careful to keep it hidden. Leastwise, careful and quiet as a stumbling drunk swerving down a pitted back road could be. There couldn't be but one way Maudie knew. *Has that devil Gaspard blood in her. Thirteen-years-old, she's already a witch. Best she be gone 'fore she curse me like her mama done.* He turned away before his daughter's hate-filled eyes could hex *him* into Marie's grave.

When night fell over the bayou, at the saloon he offered his daughter to Pascal Remillard in trade for a new pirogue, the fine canoe he'd coveted since Remillard carved it. A week later Saleau brought the widow home.

Chapter Four
The Vielle Gaspard

Maudie wasn't happy about being given to Remillard, but went with him. She couldn't stay in Saleau's house after finding her mother afloat in the bayou. *'Side's*, she thought, *gone from the old man's eye, I'll find a way to get to St. Louis. Just need time and a little money.*

Remillard was thin where Saleau was husky, but he was as mean as his father-in-law and as cheap. He counted every dime three times, and smacked her if one was missing. Laughing with Saleau at the saloon, he said, "Keepin' 'er barefoot's the bestest way to keep 'er from runnin' off."

So, Maudie stayed. There was nothing else to do.

By twenty-three she was a wet rag wrung tight till it wrinkled and dried-out. Her three front teeth were black, and her hair was like the marsh reeds behind the rotted-out four room dump Pascal Remillard brought her to on their wedding night.

Eventually the heat, the constant, dolorous steam rising from Bayou LaFit, and her husband's unabated meanness pulled her to the water's edge. Feet dangling, she cried into the bayou's heart, "*Defant Mamere*, what am I gonna do?"

The water was calm and cool on the hot afternoon. It knew her name, invited her to flee the bayou the way her mother had.

Can't. She silently fought the urge. *Got a child to see after*.

Again the water called. Still she held back until a zephyr drifted past as evening fell. The breeze carried the aroma of gumbo simmering somewhere in the bayou. It told her where refuge could be found. Remillard was out in the swamp with a jug, pretending to tend his traps. It was her chance. She bundled her daughter, Little Marie, into a pirogue and poled it to Snake Island.

"Me and the child, we're gonna stay here with you," she announced as soon as they arrived.

The *vielle* Gaspard looked deep into her niece's green eyes. "Runaway wife be an affront to God." She sighed, then nodded, as if reading the girl's heart. "I once told *votre mere* that, but she didn't… Child, hear me. You do like she done, your daughter be worse off than you. Better you stay with Remillard."

"Won't do that. Oh, *ma tante*, you just don't know—"

"Hush, child," the Swamp Witch said. "Hear me better than your ma done. Stay with him—you gotta do that. And when he's off doing what he does, you come here. Learn the Ol' Ones' hidden ways—how to use what they put on this earth to make life better."

"But—"

"Ain't no but," Lillian said. "Now come inside, we make an amulet for you to wear."

***

Maudie frequently returned to Snake Island, though it cost a beating those times Remillard came home early and she wasn't there.

"That Swamp Witch ain't gonna be teachin' you none of them devil spells," he'd growl, and pull off his belt.

Each time he smacked her, raising new welts on top of old, she heard the bayou call. And each time, fighting a desire for the peace it offered, she went back to Aunt Lillian for a balm or amulet to ease her pain. In a while, skin callused, the beatings hurt less, and Maudie's mind became as still as the bayou in August. This was the sign the *vielle* Gaspard awaited. Now she could begin to teach her niece the old ways.

The first lesson came while they prepared plots for planting herbs during the waxing moon. They ground mistletoe and sprinkled it around. On their knees, they worked it into the soil with bare hands.

"Gotta feel the earth, and let it feel you, too," Aunt Lillian Gaspard patiently instructed, then leaned back to brush unbound grey hair from her face. She wouldn't make the mistake she'd made with Marie. Maudie would learn the old ways from the earth to the pot.

Time and again they watered and worked the dark, rich ground, all the while chanting prayers to the Old Ones in hope renewed life would reward their devotion.

Skinny like her mother, though not yet wrung dry, Little Marie sat nearby while they worked. Her small hands emulating each move, she scratched out a small patch of her own.

"Life be precious, children," Aunt Lillian said, and nodded to each in turn. "Gotta give life, not take it. That's the lesson of the Ol' Ones."

Maudie scanned the *vielle* Gespard's island. Though there was respite here with her aunt, the bayou continued to call. She heard its voice in the whirring of crickets and cicadas.

Aunt Lillian grasped her face and turned it back to their work. "Life, child," she said again. "That's what we're doing here."

When twilight crept up, they built a small fire under the moon's first glow. Stars as a guide, they marked the north, east, south, and west of their bed.

"That long rope there by the shed—" Aunt Lillian pointed when the plot was mapped. "—bring it here. Tie it good, tight at the end. Mustn't be no break in it."

Little Marie held the rope while Maudie tied it tight.

"Now set it in a circle 'cross the ground," Aunt Lillian said.

Once she was satisfied with the rope border, she walked the perimeter and entered the ring from the north. Content she'd read all the signs, adhered to each detail of the ritual, she smiled blissfully to the heavens. "It's good. This garden be blessed," she sang three times, and drew a rough star across the bed with a sharp double-bladed knife.

"Did you teach *mamere* this, too?" Maudie asked.

The old woman froze. "Wish I had. Maybe then…" She shook her head, and a single tear ran down her cheek.

The next morning they carried out wicker baskets that overflowed with seedlings. In a voice surprisingly as young as the new day, old Aunt Lillian described the properties of each plant they lovingly placed in the earth.

"This here be lousewart. You put it in first 'cause it purifies, makes all your work blessed by the Ol' Ones. Need cucumber, too." She winked. "Cucumber makes you fertile."

Giggling, Maudie covered her daughter's ears. "Shouldn't oughta be saying such things 'front of the child."

Aunt Lillian pulled Little Marie close, and patted her cheek. "Your child's old enough to know what life is," she said with a soft smile. "That cucumber, it makes sure you have plenty of babies 'round to give you joy, li'l child. You hear? Then we plant this here honeystalk to protect you when you do. And this lavender, too."

Little Marie held a sprig to her nose. Her eyelids fluttering, she took in its sweet smell. "What this do?"

"Lavender takes away the fear."

Fear. The word echoed in Maudie's mind. She clutched a sprig to her breast.

The *vielle* Gaspard stroked her hand. Sounding again as old as her years, she said, "I know, child." She snipped a piece from the plant stem, and, whispering a prayer put it in the pocket of Maudie's apron.

"What are you saying?"

"Not yet. You'll know in time."

As each plant went into the ground Aunt Lillian made Maudie repeat its name and use until she knew them by heart. Little Marie echoed the words. Only then was the ceremony complete.

The old woman was right about her garden: it was exceedingly blessed. Every seedling grew full and strong. Summer brought an abundance of herbs for Maudie's gumbo pot. When each reached its season, the signs being right, Lillian led her through the garden.

"This all be property of the Ol' Ones," she warned each time. "Take more than your portion it'll make them mad, and they won't give you so much next time."

"*Oui, ma tante*," Maudie obediently responded.

Apparently satisfied the lesson was understood, Aunt Lillian said, "Gather these herbs during the waxing moon. Look out there, child, over them trees at the moon. Your heart knows the truth of things now. It'll tell you the right days."

In two years Maudie learned the time to sow and to reap. She became adept at drying herbs and spices, and at grinding them for amulets. She memorized recipes for mixing them into stews. In time she could do it all almost as well as her aunt. As confidence in her skill grew, so did a belief she could snap the strap Remillard used so often.

Aunt Lillian knows what to do. Soon I'll know, too. Then, mamere, then I'll make things right.

She needed just one thing more.

One day they were in the dark kitchen of the *vielle* Gaspard's hut, vegetables from their garden piled on a rough wood table near the stove. They were cooking a recipe Lillian Gaspard called Witches Gumbo. Sitting on a high stool, Little Marie chanted, "Onion, pepper, celery; slice, dice the trinity…"

Maudie rested her knife on the table, and wiped sweat from her brow. Without looking at her aunt, she asked, "Whilst I cook this, what do I say to make a man crazy mad?"

The *vielle* Gaspard shuddered. Knowing Maudie's heart, she feared where the answer might lead.

"*Ma tante*, what words do I say?" Maudie asked again, daring a quick glance up.

"That's not what it's for!" Aunt Lillian shook a gnarled finger. "Do that, it'll bring three times the madness on you."

Maudie averted her eyes. "No *ma tante*. I wouldn't. Just… wanna know if I could."

Lillian wasn't fooled. Knowing the cost, still the girl wanted magic for revenge. *Against life that takes everything, and gives nothing*, she thought. As if she'd heard her niece's silent cry, the *vielle* Gaspard muttered, "Luc Saleau, Pascal Remillard, you've done this."

For all her skill, she understood she'd never douse the fire in Maudie's heart. Still she tried. Even as she lay dying, she warned, "Whatever you do child, both the good and bad of it, comes back to you three times."

The Swamp Witch's words went unheeded. When Maudie walked from the grave after Aunt Lillian's funeral song was sung, a crooked smile darted across her face. Had anyone seen, they'd have known the look meant she was now free of restraint and ready to act.

Luc Saleau would be first. He'd started it all—was responsible for *defante mamere's* death and her life with Remillard.

The moon was right, the signs were all present. Saleau was now a gray bearded old man who did little but fish, hunt, and complain. Sober, he was crude. Drunk he was cruel, and he was constantly drunk. Not even his new wife cared much for him any longer. Maudie was certain no one would mark or mind his disappearance. It wouldn't take much to tip the damn pirogue for which she'd been traded, only the ingestion of the right herbal mixture. The bayou would do the rest.

Chapter Five
The Bayou

Bayou LaFit gathered for a feast just before Lent. They sat on folding chairs and time-stained white wicker on the narrow patch of ground between Remillard's house and the swamp. Near the screened-in porch, a fiddle and guitar sang in counterpoint to the Cajun cadence of a washtub bass.

Cooking was the one thing Pascal Remillard admitted his wife did well. Leaning back in his chair, he unbuttoned the sweat-stained denim shirt that strained to hold his stomach, and announced, "Ain't no one down by this bayou make a gumbo good's my Maudie. Just look at this belly."

He grinned contentedly, and lifted his undershirt and rubbed the mat of hair which seemed more animal than human. He took no notice of his wife's sunken eyes and the way her cheekbones almost pushed through drawn skin. He took no pride in her, just in the way she could turn anything he shot or trapped into a sumptuous meal.

"Prideful of his possession, he is," Pere Bonifay remarked, pulling at his black cassock and holding up a hand to fend off such a sin. "Yes, Remillard's grown far too fat for his britches."

Dr. Billiot nodded, and looked out over the bayou. "Man's got the gumbo, all right." The aged doctor and priest were two of many partaking of the meal Maudie put out that Fat Tuesday.

Luc Saleau had also come to the feast—Maudie's… special guest.

"*Ici, mon pere*," she stroked the old man's shoulder. Dutifully, she refilled his bowl. "You're not looking too well. Just a tetch of this file fix you up good." Without expression, she sprinkled a pinch of the gray-green powdered sassafras bark into his stew.

Saleau laughed. To Remillard, he said, "Well, well. Looks like you done good work taming that devil."

"Just needed showing her right place." Remillard laughed, too. The day was fine. The nut-brown gumbo was thick with game, okra, and herbs. His wife was obedient. There wasn't but one more thing a man could want. "Woman, I be needing another beer," he commanded, and beckoned to Maudie with his empty bottle.

She rushed off, returning in a moment with a fresh one.

When night fell Saleau rowed into Bayou LaFit. No one knew why he felt compelled to check his traps in the swampy darkness. Seemed like once an idea came into his head there was no stopping the old man until he'd acted on it. So he turned his pirogue into the swamp as midnight neared, and didn't return.

***

Two days later, Sheriff Granbeede shifted his large bottom in a chair outside the saloon. "Might oughta go looking for where some jug of shine dumped that bastard Saleau's drunken carcass," he said to Dr. Billiot.

"Sure you want to?" The doctor grinned and pulled the wire rimmed glasses from his veined nose. "Been nice and quiet without that braggart heating things up."

The hefty, gray-suited sheriff sighed. "Best be doing it anyways. Oughta know where he built his still this time."

After a day of poling through the bayou, the sheriff found the pirogue afloat in drowned duckweed near Snake Island, a half-empty moonshine jug propped against coiled rope inside it. There was no sign of Saleau.

"Looks like that somebitch just tipped out," Granbeede told Dr. Billiot when he returned. "Some gator must've had him some good gumbo just afore Lent."

"I suppose you're right," the doctor said. "One day somebody gonna catch the gator what ate Saleau, find his belt or boot in its belly."

Granbeede tilted back in his chair. For a passing moment he wondered if the file powder Maudie sprinkled in Saleau's bowl had something to do with what happened to the old man. Had she sweetened anyone else's gumbo from the same jar? He couldn't remember. Either way, there wasn't much he'd do about it. Only fools chased after gators—or worse, tried to wrestle a polecat who might know one or two of her great-aunt's spells.

Much better to have another beer, and see what comes about, he thought, knowing something would. In Bayou LaFit it always did.

The townsfolk also chewed a bit on the unexplained disappearance. After all, Saleau had been raised in the bayou, knew its every twist and turn. Never before had a jug of moonshine made him careless of its moods. When someone swore she'd seen Maudie and her daughter singing and spreading flower petals by the bayou's bank the night he vanished, what but witchcraft could they conclude?

The talk didn't last long. In the end, the idea of songs, flowers, and spices tipping the old man from his boat was too much gumbo for anyone to swallow.

Chapter Six
Pascal

Pascal Remillard took no warning from the unexplained disappearance. Not even after he found a rag doll—dressed in the same torn undershirt and stained slacks Saleau always wore—behind some kindling near the icebox on the screened porch.

"What's this business here?" He waved the doll in Maudie's face. "This one of the Swamp Witch spells?"

Stand quiet, she told herself. *This'll soon be over*.

"Good thing that *vielle* Gaspard's worm food," Remillard shouted, his face as scarlet as the scarf around his neck. He pulled the doll back then raised it as if ready to strike his wife. "Wasn't dead, I'd take Pere Bonifay, go there to Snake Island, burn her out and all her witch evil with her." Since this was no longer possible, he gave Maudie a single blow with the back of his hand, and stormed off.

She hissed like a coiled snake at his back, but quickly cooled her anger. Nothing could be done about him during Lent. What she had in mind would be a sin during those holy days. Even after Lent ended, she had to await the proper omens. They came in early May.

***

Little Marie dropped a dish towel.

"Guess we're gonna have company today," Maudie gave voice to the local superstition.

Immediately she lit the stove under her gumbo pot. From a wood box beneath her bed, she gathered a handful of dried rosemary, cumin, henbane, and a precious pinch of lavender. She looked at her lousewart—an ingredient that would purify her mixture—but shook her head.

No need for this. Can't purify that man. Her small laugh was a sigh of relief.

This was her final task, the end of a circle which began with Saleau and her *defant mamere. No need to reckon past that*, she thought, and closed the box.

In a small stone bowl the *vielle* Gaspard had given her, she carefully ground the herbs to release their essential oils, then combined them with her file powder.

Little Marie's eyes went wide when the jar was capped and placed in the apron covering Maudie's gingham dress. "*Mamere*—" She tugged at her mother's arm. "—Aunt Lillian said you dasn't—"

"Hush, child."

"But, *mamere*—"

"Hush," Maudie whispered, and held her daughter close. *Whatever you do, both the good and bad of it, comes back*, she heard the *vielle* Gaspard warn. These words had hovered over her each day since her father disappeared. *Saleau, Remillard, mamere, me*: it seemed their circle was filled with tears. With a quick motion, she wiped her eyes. "Hush," she said again to her daughter. And to herself. "This'll soon be done, and I won't do it again."

In the afternoon the Widow Saleau dropped by with fresh vegetables from her garden. Remillard saw the Model-T pull up. Not inclined to sit anywhere nearby through an afternoon of women-talk, he dug out his squirrel gun.

Maudie stopped him at the door. "Ain't gonna be unsociable are you? Least you could do's stay for some gumbo and ice tea 'fore you run off."

Remillard turned and looked longingly into the swamp beyond the duckweed. He could already taste the bite of liquor from the still he'd built out there. Yet, the heady aroma wafting from Maudie's pot drew him back. With a grunt, he rested his rifle against the rotted slats of the porch wall, and dropped into a large wicker chair by the Widow's side.

"You'll have some, too?" Maudie said to their guest. "Just go to waste if you don't. And waste even after

Lent's a prideful sin." She pulled the small jar from her apron, and shook a bit of the powder over the gumbo in both bowls.

Remillard grabbed her arm. "What's that there? Think you're gonna make me gator food, too?"

"This?" Maudie showed him the jar. "It's just some file." Her face showing innocent surprise, she wiped her hands down the sides of her stained dress. "It goes fine in the gumbo. Makes it all the sweeter."

Remillard rubbed his pointed jaw and eyed his wife. *Nothing but ragged bones, what could that sow do to me?* Still, after what folks said when Luc Saleau disappeared, could he trust the powder she put in that jar? The rich, earthy smell when it hit his gumbo was irresistible. "What the hell," he said at last. "Just a spoonful or two can't hurt."

In the end, he finished every morsel in his bowl. So did the Widow Saleau. They both used slices of fresh-baked *miche,* a thick crusty bread, to sop the dregs.

"Why Maudie, I do believe that's the best gumbo you ever made," the Widow said, her eyelids batting when she handed the bowl back. "Don't you think so Pascal, dear?"

She sighed when she called Pascal *dear*, and he returned a salacious, lip-licking smile.

Leave them alone now, Maudie thought. *Let the gumbo make him want her*. Rising, she said, "Better go wash these bowls, put the rest of the gumbo in the icebox 'fore it's spoilt."

Standing quietly just inside the kitchen, Maudie listened to her husband and the Widow. At first their talk was soft, gentle. Remillard's voice almost crooned. *Soon this'll all be done with, and me and Little Marie can run off to St. Louis, see the fair.* She held her breath.

Within moments the voices were raised to shouts. Chairs scraped along the wood floor.

"What you doing!" the Widow cried.

"Just a little sweetness—"

"Stop!"

"Just a touch of your sweet breasts—"

"No!" The word was punctuated by a shot from the squirrel gun.

Maudie slipped out the door of the screened porch.

The Widow stood by an overturned wicker chair. One hand covered her mouth, the other held the rifle with smoke floating from its barrel. Remillard was a lump on the ground at her feet. A red stain oozed from where his heart had been.

"He…" the Widow began. "He just… climbing all over me… dirty paws up inside my dress. Don't know what made it happen." Her shock turned to tears, and she uttered, *"Mais, ja'mais d'la vie!"*

Maudie took Remillard's squirrel gun from the woman's trembling hands. "Best I send the child for Doctor Billiot. You just set here till he comes."

But, she didn't send her daughter just yet. First, her eyes clouded, she looked down at what was left of her husband. "White gulls and herons, take this poor sinner's soul," she chanted. "Make it pure 'fore the earth takes it home." She closed her eyes. Though her lips still moved there was no sound.

Little Marie held her hand, and chanted along.

At last Maudie looked up. "Go quick child, find Doctor Billiot. Tell him *votre pere* been shot."

Little Marie raced the two miles to the Five Corners. She found the doctor in the shade of the wood porch outside the saloon, his chair cocked back against the clapboard wall next to Sheriff Granbeede. At ease in a comfortable silence, the two men pulled on beers while they watched gulls loop lazily over the cypress trees.

"D… doctor," Little Marie panted. *"Mamere…* she says you gotta come right off. The Widow Saleau… she… shot *mon pere."*

The sheriff's chair thudded forward, its front legs banging on the porch under his considerable weight. "What's this?"

"She done it. The Widow done it. He's lying on the ground bleeding."

Doctor Billiot reached for the bag at his feet. "Why'd she do that?"

Little Marie pulled at her dress. "Dunno. He said something to her, and she just... done it."

Sheriff Granbeede leaned back again, his eyelids flickering. After a moment he took a long swallow from his bottle, and licked his lips. "I'm thinking maybe I might oughta ride along, you don't mind," he said to Billiot.

Chapter Seven
The Widow

When the doctor and the sheriff arrived, Remillard's body looked as though all his years of drink, food, and fight had been sucked out. The Widow was still in tears.

"What happened here?" the sheriff demanded of her.

"He just... he... he just... all over me," she moaned, and repeated the same thing in answer to every question.

The widow was badly in need of sedation, and Granbeede knew he'd get no more from her. Nothing for it, all they could do was pronounce Pascal Remillard quite dead, and haul the widow and body back to town.

Dosed on laudanum, on a bed in back of Doctor Billiot's house the Widow Saleau tried to explain why she'd shot Pascal Remillard. "Ate that gumbo Maudie gave us, me and... and..." she murmured. "Can't reckon much after. Except, the way... he was looking at me so... it was his eyes!"

"Said you had some gumbo Maudie Remillard cooked up?" The sheriff nodded. "Put something in it, did she—powder from a little jar she keeps in her apron?"

More than half asleep, the widow ran her tongue across dry lips. "Y... y..." she tried to say, but could only nod before her eyes closed and she began to snore.

Doctor Billiot shot a strange look at the sheriff. "You're not thinking—"

"Uh-huh."

Billiot's grey brow furrowed. He pulled off his glasses. "The widow? Surely—"

The sheriff shook his head. "Maudie."

"But, how?"

"The gumbo. I allow as how it might've done old Luc Saleau, too."

The doctor gave him a myopic stare. "Murder—"

"Could be." Granbeede nodded.

"—by gumbo?" Billiot almost choked on the word.

"Heard of stranger things happening down by this bayou. Folks used to say such things 'bout the Swamp Witch. I'm thinking I might oughta stop by, talk a bit to Maudie Remillard tomorrow morning. Get things in the open.

The matter might have ended there—some questions, an arrest or maybe not—if the doctor hadn't felt a need to laugh about foolish superstitions that night in the saloon. In Bayou LaFit belief in the old ways ran deep.

The idea of witchery put in their heads, the next morning half the men in town showed up at the Remillard place to see Granbeede capture the witch. A few women also came. After hearing what happened to Remillard, folks recalled rumors about Maudie dressed in white by the bayou the night her father vanished, and were convinced both deaths began and ended with her.

"Hadda be evil witchery Maudie brewed up in her gumbo pot, made poor old Luc disappear," they said, sounding fonder of him now he was dead.

"And kept anyone from knowing what she done till she fed some to Pascal, too," they agreed."

"Witchery's what it's gotta be."

"Get out here witch! Answer what you done," someone shouted to the silent shack.

In the crowd's yell, Maudie again heard the *vielle* Gaspard say, *Whatever you do comes back...* "I know that, *ma tante*," she whispered to the memory. "But, St. Louis is so far. Wasn't no other way to get there."

"Get the witch out here!" the town bellowed.

Maudie replied with her husband's squirrel gun: a sharp crack followed an echoed whine as the bullet whizzed over everyone's head. The mob scattered to a safe distance. In the gun's voice she again heard her aunt say, *The good and the bad, it all comes back.*

Little Marie ran crying between the rooms. "*Mamere, mamere*—"

"Hush child," Maudie said while she reloaded the gun.

The angry crowd's curses and threats rushed through the window.

"What we gonna do?" Little Marie moaned.

The Swamp Witch's voice floated in on a breeze from the bayou. *Three times. Saleau, Remillard. The Ol' Ones demand three.*

Maudie dried her daughter's tears with a corner of her apron, and gently kissed the child's forehead. She'd do what she had to, what she should've known it would come to the day she found her *defant mamere* face-down in the swamp. "Hush li'l one," she crooned, using the apron to dry her own tears. "*Votre mere* won't let these people hurt you."

"But, *mamere*—"

Maudie placed a finger on the child's lips, then put a wicker basket into her hands and pushed her away. "Go now. Go fast."

Little Marie looked over her shoulder, frightened.

"Git!" Maudie said, and turned the squirrel gun out the window.

***

𝒟ucking the wild shot, none of the huddled townsfolk saw a small figure slip from the house and run to the duckweed at the water's edge. The screen door's slam was lost in the sound of a second crack and an echoed whine.

The Widow Saleau stood up, adjusted her skirt, and marched to Granbeede. Hands on her ample hips, she said, "She done it to me—fixed a *cunja* with that powder she made. Get in there, bring out the witch!"

The sheriff took a step back.

Doctor Billiot laughed. "Y'ain't afraid of no hex, are you?"

"Hex, bullet, same thing. Be just as dead," Granbeede groaned. "Where's Pere Bonifay? He can talk her outta there."

Before the priest could be summoned, someone shouted, "Don't need him. Fire will do the trick."

"Yeah! Burn the witch out," another voice raged. Others took up the chant. A lit match was dropped on dry grass.

The sheriff's head swiveled. "This ain't the way," he rasped.

"It's the onliest way," someone answered.

Maudie appeared in the window with the squirrel gun raised. "Git from my property, 'fore I fix a *cunja* on all of you!" she shouted.

"Stop them," Billiot called to Granbeede.

Another shot came from the house. Maudie's face was again in the window. "Git I said!"

She knew her defiance would make the vaporous morning hotter. She'd done what she'd done. Now the Old Ones demanded the circle be closed.

"Burn the witch out!" the townsfolk screamed. Rags were wrapped around a broken cypress branch, and kindled. "Burn the witch!"

"Stop this, all of you," Dr. Billiot pleaded. "Witchcraft had nothing to do—" His voice was drowned by the mob's shouts.

At the doctor's side, Granbeede made one last try. Reaching a hand towards the torchbearer, he demanded, "Give it here!"

The man waved the torch in his face. "Gonna take it?"

Maudie reached through the window and upended her jar of file. The powder scattered on the ground.

"She's hexing us," somebody cried. "Get her, get the witch!"

"Stop this. Stop this. Sheriff, do something!" Billiot yelled.

Granbeede shook his head. "Uh-uh. I ain't crossing over that hex dust."

Again the crack of the squirrel gun sounded from the house. The town ducked.

The sheriff cocked his head to listen. Something was different: the shot was duller; there'd been no stinging whine overhead. He stared at the empty window. *That shot weren't sent at us*, he thought, and shook his head. He knew who this bullet was for. *Damn, Maudie, what you done?*

"Burn the witch, 'fore she shoots someone," the Widow said.

"Get her 'fore someone's killed," the mob echoed.

Granbeede grabbed the torch. *No matter now*, he thought, and tossed it at the porch. It broke through the screen, and lay for a moment on the bare wood floor.

The townsfolk looked on in silence as a gentle, cloying breeze blew off the bayou. It passed over the lit torch, and urged the fire toward a straw mat. From there a spark flew to the window curtain, and crawled up to the roof. In moments the house was in flames. Dry timber popped, crackled, and turned to ash. Beams collapsed, the walls fell in.

A gasp rose from the duckweed while the fire gnawed its meal. No one heard it. They were too absorbed by the sight of the flames to allow a thought for Little Marie. So the child remained hidden at the bayou's edge, her eyes red, yanking her hair while she moaned, "Mamere, mamere, no!"

After a while the Widow pulled her eyes from the smoking house, and turned to Dr. Billiot. Arms wrapped defiantly around her chest, she demanded, "Don't hear her crying, do you? Isn't no crying. Fire don't hurt her. That proves she's a witch."

"She's guilty of witchery, all right," someone answered—a juror rendering the post-mortem verdict.

"The law's satisfied, right sheriff?" another said.

Staring at his hands, Granbeede didn't answer.

"Well, doctor?" The Widow Saleau asked.

Billiot walked away without a word.

When the fire finally ate its fill, Bayou LaFit spit and peed on the embers. "That there finishes the circle of witchery in this bayou," somebody snorted, and kicked at Maudie's smoldering corpse.

Her face streaked with tears, from the tall bayou reeds Little Marie watched everyone leave. Then, her jaw set in the determined way she'd learned from her mother, she slipped her basketful of lavender and okra into a pirogue, and poled it out to Snake Island.

Captive Soul

Manic laughter has chased Emily since she was ten and climbed through the window of an abandoned house. Could this laughter be the voice of a ghost which attached itself to her that day?

Like CNN headlines, the manic laughter scrolls across the screen of my mind. The shrink sitting at the other side of the table with an open file and pages scattered, doesn't believe in ghosts. My fear talking, he calls it. But, this man with little compassion in his eyes wasn't there the first time I heard it. Or the other times. No, he wasn't with the ten year-old girl who wiggled through a window of an abandoned house on a corner in the place I grew up.

"Tell me again," he says.

I don't want to recall it. Yet, I do.

***

Main Street stretched for miles from Northern Boulevard in Flushing to Jamaica Avenue. My piece of it was a twelve block section of Queens called Kew Gardens Hills. My friends and I knew every crack in the pavement along those blocks, from the deli where we bought grilled hot dogs and pickles, to the one-screen theater where Saturday afternoons found us in the front row, watching Godzilla devour Tokyo with as much gusto as we ate popcorn. Horror films were our favorites. With our eyes wide discs, we would push back in our seats while monsters and evil spirits seized the souls of unsuspecting victims. We enjoyed being scared. Until that day.

As we left the deli, pickles in hand, Eddie Marks had an idea.

"They're showing a Hopalong Cassidy movie today." He curled his lip. "It's Halloween, don't wanna see cowboys."

"What else is there?" Pam asked.

He watched a city bus pass the movie theater, pass Sam's Candy Store and O'Malley's butcher shop. "The house," he said.

Where the bus stopped across the street from the Episcopal Church, stood a derelict wood-framed structure. Two badly weathered stories, slats rotting on the wrap-around porch, and the roof hanging by a few shingles in spots, this house was a neighborhood legend. The ghost of its murdered owner roamed its rooms, moaning with the wind on stormy nights. Cold fingers grabbed the living who dared to enter, and closed on their throats. Tight. Tighter. Squeezing, until they died.

At least, that's what high school kids told us. They also said the priest from the church tried to exorcize the ghost, but ran from the house, ashen-faced, when it laughed at him.

Believing these stories, I stopped with my pickle half-way to my mouth. "Uh-uh. Not going in there. No way!"

"Yes, way," Eddie said. He had crew-cut blond hair, and a round face with a pug nose, set on a barrel body. A year older than I, he was the kind of kid that tore his shirt scaling the chain link fence around our school, and straddled the bar twenty feet up laughing at the rest of us. Eddie feared nothing.

Pam pulled on her brown braid. "I... don't know..."

What are ya, sissies?" Ken Hoffmann slapped a hand on Eddie's shoulder. "I'm with ya, even if these *girls* aren't."

"Who are you calling girls?" Did he think I was a wussy? "Okay, I'll go," I said, sounding anything but sure I wanted to.

"Not me." Pam glanced at Eddie and Ken. "I... uh, all the filth and spider webs in there." She brushed the front of her blouse. "My mom'll kill me if I come home dirty."

My mother wouldn't be angry if I came home dirty. Half the time Mom didn't know where I was. And Dad...

"Ain't afraid of a little ghost, are ya?" Eddie laughed. "There ain't such things."

"I know. But..." Pam shook her head, and walked away.

How different my life might have been if I'd gone with her.

***

The green trim on the porch railings and around the windows and door was chipped and faded. The siding had fallen away from places on the walls, leaving torn tarpaper to face the elements. The door and windows were boarded. Scattered pieces of wood on the unmown, weed-filled lawn might at one time have been window shutters. The three stairs creaked, and a decayed slat cracked as Ken stepped onto the porch.

"Oh, shit!" he said, reaching to retrieve the sneaker which had been pulled from his foot. "How'd that happen?"

Eddie gave me a tight-lipped smile. To Ken, he said, "Must've been the ghost, untied your shoe."

He led us along the porch, looking for a way to get in. At last, he found a window where the boards were loose enough to squeeze through.

Inside, we were in a small, dank room, the walls covered by gray paper adorned with tiny roses. Light crept through cracks between the boards on the window, and crawled along the dust-filled floor. Cobwebs filled every corner. A crow cawed from beyond the closed door.

I glanced around. Eddie was grinning. Ken wasn't.

"Let's see what's on the other side of that door," Eddie said, and reached for the knob.

Something creaked. Footsteps slowly approached the door. I heard them. Clomp, creak, clomp, creak.

"Don't open it!" I shouted.

"What're afraid of?" Eddie said.

"Didn't you hear—?"

"Hear what?" Ken said.

Now I heard pounding on the door.

"Don't you hear that?

"What?" Eddie said.

A hand grabbed my leg. I screamed, and ran.

Laughter filled the room as I slithered through the slats on the window, and scampered from the porch.

I don't know whether Ken and Eddie followed me out. I didn't look back, didn't stop running until I reached my house and closed my bedroom door. On my bed, pushed against the wall with a pillow held tightly to my chest, I still heard the low, crazed *Aaaaaaahaahaa.*

Books I've read since that day, warn against ghost hunting. They say spirits can attach themselves to a person. Because of what's happened since, I believe it.

***

My family lived in a two-story attached house. I was doing homework in my bedroom, when I heard raised voices.

"Damn ballgames! You gonna watch it all night?" Mom shouted. She always sounded annoyed.

"Aw, hell, what now?" Dad yelled back.

A cabinet door opened and slammed shut. Ice cubes clinked in a glass. "I could use help here." Mom's words were slurred.

"In a minute!"

"I work my tail off, and with him it's always in a minute," Mom said loud enough for him to hear. Loud enough for the neighborhood to hear.

I slammed my bedroom door, leaned against it, and held my breath. At seventeen, I didn't need to hear them go at it again. My room was small, sparsely furnished: a bed, a desk by the single window covered by a blind with broken slats, a dresser, and stained carpeting.

Downstairs, my parents' tempers flared, a fire out of control. Behind my closed door I could almost ignore them.

Laughter seeped under my door. *Aaaaahaahaa.*

"Who's there?"

No one answered.

I cracked open the door, peeked into the hall. It was empty. My brother's room was empty. It must have been the ghost that followed me from house by the church. Damn my mother, my father: they're the reason it had hung around. For seven years I'd heard the laughter each time they began to fight. I turned up the volume of my stereo. Through the speakers, Bonnie Raitt wailed, *I can't make you love me*—

Mom's voice was shrill. It cut through the closed door as if the wood were cardboard. It rose over the music.

"Every day it's the same damn thing!" she said. "You shovel dinner down your throat like you can't wait to get outta here. Then you plop like a lump of lard in front of the damn TV all night."

Dad shouted, "I work my ass off at the lot all day! Is it too much to want peace when I get home?"

"My dream man. Instead of a prince, I got a used car salesman and a pile of bills we can't pay. We're gonna lose our house, be out on the street!"

Aahahaaa.

I crawled onto my bed, pillow around my ears. It didn't help.

Mom again: "You might as well not be here, Lou. You hear me?"

Dad again: "Aw, hell, why do I try?"

Heavy footsteps moved toward the front door.

"You don't try, that's your problem! Sure, go ahead, leave. You're not here when you're here. What difference does it make?"

The screen door squeaked.

"Go on—run off to your friends in that greasy bar!" Mom yelled.

He didn't answer.

From the front stoop, she shouted, "You'll be back!"

Dad's voice came through my bedroom window. "Not this time!"

The car door slammed.

Aaahaaa.

"Stop it, stop it!" I screamed at the damn ghost. At my parents. I wanted to run from the house, not stop until I was with my boyfriend. I couldn't, though. Eddie was a waiter at summer camp.

"Why aren't you here when I need you?" I cried to the thought of him. I felt trapped in my room, in my life.

Aahaha.

It was night now. Dad hadn't come home. Mom sat at the kitchen table crying to a glass of scotch. At my desk, bent over my diary, I wrote a life-plan. Bulleted points: Go to Harvard Law School; Marry Eddie (wedding reception at the Plaza); Work for a Wall Street law firm that pays lots of money; Have a baby; Buy a colonial house in the suburbs (ten rooms on a one acre plot, with a swing set out back); Another baby; Spend my life surrounded by my husband and children.

The laughter began again, loud, long. *Aahaaaaaaa.*

I jumped into bed, covers over my head.

***

Ten years later I was in the small kitchen of the garden apartment Eddie and I lived in, one of many in a large complex near the Long Island Expressway. My life-plan was working out: I'd become a lawyer, married him—not a wedding at the Plaza as I'd dreamed, yet I was a Mrs. and now I was pregnant. I held a cookbook open on a shelf with one hand while I reached across to the refrigerator with the other. When I opened the door, a dozen eggs floated out. They didn't splatter on the floor. The cardboard carton lifted, turned, opened. Eggs flew across the room, smacked against the cabinets. One broke on my forehead.

Laughter drifted down from the ceiling.

I dropped the mixing bowl. My legs gave. I crumbled to the floor, clutching the cookbook to my chest. "Eddie!" I cried.

My husband had grown a foot since the Halloween we climbed into the haunted house, he'd slimmed down, and though he still had a pug nose, his hair was longer and now dirty blond.

"Dinner ready?" he called from the living room.

"Get in here!"

"Just a minute—the inning's almost over."

"Now!"

Grumbling with annoyance, he padded around the wall to the kitchen, and nearly doubled-over at the sight. "Emily, I know you're just learning how to cook. But, if you read the instructions, the eggs go in a bowl not on you and the walls."

"You didn't hear?"

My mind flashed back seventeen years when he said, "Hear what?"

We ate at a restaurant that night, a tarnished pleasure since my husband wanted everyone to know about the flying eggs.

"A ghost in our kitchen? More likely a ghost in my wife's little head," he chuckled to the waitress when she brought our meal.

He still laughed about it while we drove home after dinner. When we pulled up to our apartment block, he said, "Hey, I know. Maybe it's the ghost of your cousin Fred who died in the Trade Towers. Didn't you tell me he always threw snowballs at you when you were kids? Snowballs, eggs—" He made a weighing motion with his hands. "Yeah, could be. Good old Fred was always a joker. Figures he'd come back as a poltergeist."

I leaned against the passenger-side door and held tight to the handle, biting my lip. Could Eddie be any more insensitive? What happened to the man I married, the one who vowed to cherish and protect me? The one who couldn't wait for the reception to be over so he could get into my pants? Two years past our wedding, I hardly recognized him. Since high school, we'd never dated anyone else. We were so young when we met, I'd thought that's what love is. These days, I felt as if I were no more than a source of amusement for him. Had I rushed him into marriage so I could get away from my mother's drinking? No, I could have moved out her house any time I wanted. Of course, I had school loans to repay—that would have made it difficult—

I looked up at our apartment. A shadow moved past the window. I trembled. Evil lurked in there, I was sure of it. I didn't want to climb the three flights, didn't want to unlock our door, didn't want find out what or who the shadow might be. But, I had nowhere else to go.

Aahaaa. The laughter came from the back seat.

Afraid to look, I grabbed Eddie's arm. "Didn't you hear that?"

"Not this again." He shook his head.

"Yes! It's here… in the car—"

He laughed at me. "Old Cousin Fred's still rattling around in your brain, huh?"

My husband wasn't quite so smug the next night when Pam and Ken Hoffmann came over for dinner, though he started out that way.

I had just finished washing the dishes when I heard laughter in the living room. Though it didn't sound the same, I froze. When I could move again, I hesitantly leaned around the kitchen wall. "What's… going on?"

"I was telling them about your kitchen helper," Eddie said with a snide grin. "You know, Emily, your ghost."

As if someone sneaked up behind me, the hairs stood up on the nape of my neck. I threw the dishtowel into the sink and ran for the living room.

Pam and Ken lounged on the sofa. My husband was in an armchair next to them, his legs stretched out on the coffee table. Embarrassed by both my husband and my fear, I whined, "It isn't funny. Come on guys, don't laugh at me. I was scared silly."

Eddie chuckled. "Certainly silly. I'm not so sure your breaking a dozen eggs is scary, though. Unless—" he mocked horror "—you're throwing them at me with that look in your eyes."

I perched on the armrest of the sofa.

Pam put her arm around my shoulders. "You shouldn't pick on her." She patted my cheek. "Men—they're all alike. Everything's a joke to them."

"Thank you," I said. "At least you understand."

Her long, brown hair shook when she laughed. "Still, you have to admit it's funny—the idea of a poltergeist heaving eggs across your kitchen. Do you think you could keep it as a pet? I wonder what poltergeists eat."

"You, too?" I pushed her away.

"Hey, ease up," Pam said. "There isn't a ghost in your house—there aren't such things. And I've got news for you: there's no tooth fairy, either."

"And no Santa," Eddie said.

"Really?" Pam faked a gasp.

The guys laughed.

While I pouted, a light in the unfinished nursery turned on. I saw the glow down the short hallway. The light flickered twice, a third time, then went out.

I reached for my husband. "Uh, Eddie…"

He leaned away. "Come on, Emily, It's just a lose bulb or something."

The light flickered again.

"It isn't!" I was shaking.

"You're being ridiculous," Eddie said.

The light flickered a last time then died.

"Eddie, stop it!" Pam smacked his arm. "Ghost or no ghost, can't you see she's terrified?"

He rolled his eyes. "There's nothing to be frightened of. Look, I'll show you." He pulled his legs from the coffee table, rose, and took two steps toward the nursery.

"Don't! Eddie, please don't go in there," I cried.

"Why? You're just being a girl about this." He gave Ken's shoulder a good-natured punch. "C'mon, let's show her."

"You don't understand—it isn't the bulb."

"Of course it is," the guys insisted.

"It's not!"

They looked at each other, and Eddie said, "Okay, electrician, how do you know?"

"That bulb burned out last night. I removed it, but didn't replace it because I forgot to buy spares."

My husband laughed at me. I felt as though a traitor inhabited his heart.

"You're always forgetting something," he said. Then, what I told him finally penetrated his skull. "Hey, wait a minute. No bulb? Impossible."

He and Ken went to investigate.

"What's wrong?" Pam asked when they returned.

Ken pulled at his beard. "She's right. There's no bulb in the lamp."

"Must have been a car's headlights bouncing off the walls or something," Eddie said, his snide complacency gone. "Yeah, that has to be it. Nothing to worry about."

I wasn't reassured and within weeks things got a lot worse.

I felt vulnerable in my home. The ghost was there, in the kitchen, in what would be my baby's room. Its laughter echoed those nights Eddie worked late and I was alone—he had moved up in his firm, and often worked late. The hoarse laughter crawled along the walls, seeped under the doors. I heard it in the hiss of the radiators. There was a curse was on my home, on Eddie, on me—the more the ghost laughed, the more certain I became.

"I can't live here anymore," I said one night during dinner. "We've got to find another apartment."

Eddie screwed up his face. "Why do you always start on me just when I'm putting the first forkful of food in my mouth?"

"Because we never talk any other time."

"Uh-huh." He stared at his plate.

"I can't, Eddie, I... I don't want to stay here."

"You were afraid of the neighborhood we left, insisted we had to move when you got pregnant. Now you're afraid of *this* apartment? We can't keep moving every time your imagination goes haywire."

"It's not my imagination. There's really something ... evil here."

He slammed down his fork. "Come on, Em. You're pregnant. Everyone knows pregnant women's hormones make them nuts. Call your doctor. Ask for some pills or something."

His words were a knife slashing the seams of our marriage. It finally tore open when my pregnancy neared the end of its eighth month.

Though I was a thin girl, I carried quite large. My back constantly ached. My ankles swelled, then my wrists. I was tired all the time, some days not able to get out of bed. At last month's prenatal examination, the doctor told me I had to start my maternity leave immediately. This put pressure on our finances.

"Gotta work late," Eddie announced the morning everything fell apart. He me gave a perfunctory kiss, and pulled on his camelhair coat.

"Not again," I groaned. What was he doing all those nights he didn't come home? Drinking with friends? Another woman? Suspicion crawled like a tarantula up my spine. Its poison touch filled me with fear. What if Eddie left me?

Aahaa, the manic disembodied voice wheezed.

"Gotta do it, Em."

"Can you at least stop for some groceries on your way home? Here's the list." I tried to hand it to him.

He brushed my arm away. "Sorry, don't know how late I'll be. Get to the store yourself."

I glared at him, tears in my eyes.

Aaaahaaaaaaa. The laughter grew louder, lasted longer.

"Dammit, do something for yourself instead of laying around all day!"

My eyes overflowed. "I can't." I spread my arms to show the mess pregnancy had made of my body. "Look at me!"

As if detesting what he saw, his eyes flicked to the apartment door. "Don't know what to tell you, Em. If you won't go out, you'd better find out if the market delivers."

I tried to shove the door closed. He jammed it open with his foot.

"This isn't fair! I'm stuck in here while you're out—"

He didn't want to hear it. As he slammed the door behind him, he said, "Someone's gotta bring in the bucks to keep this family going!"

The laughter rang in the hall outside. How could he not hear it?

That afternoon I noticed blood in my panties. I telephoned the obstetrician. He instructed me to get to the hospital. He would meet me there in a half hour.

I telephoned Eddie. His extension was busy.

Aahahaaaaaa.

I dialed again. This time his secretary answered. "Beverly, is my husband there?" I asked.

"He's in a meeting, Emily," she said coolly.

"I need him, Beverly. Get him!" A sharp needle shot from my chest to my abdomen. "NOW!"

Aahahaaaaaa.

Eddie came on the line. Obviously, he'd been in his office all along. "What is it now?" He sounded impatient.

"I'm staining."

I heard him breathing.

"Eddie?"

"Call the doctor, and call me back."

"I already spoke to him. Do you think I'm an absolute idiot?"

"Not absolute." His laughter mixed with the ghostly wheeze, became one with it, swelled until it filled every inch of the apartment. The walls closed in. I felt as though hands were squeezing my throat. I struggled for air.

"The doctor said I have to get to the hospital right away." I groaned when another pang doubled me over.

The laughter was at my feet. Now it inched up my leg.

"I'm in an important meeting here," Eddie said. "I'll be home soon as I can. Hang in there. I'm sure nothing's really so wrong another couple of minutes will matter."

Though his office was but a few miles away, getting home took him two hours. By then I was lying in a small pool of blood. Pam Hoffman was beside me, trying to lift me into a sitting position.

"Nice of you to get here, sport," she hissed at Eddie.

"What happened?" His face was blank, the image of innocence.

"While you were deciding whether to bother coming home, Emily called me. Good thing she did. She passed out while I was phoning for an ambulance."

Emergency Services arrived just then. Fifteen minutes later, two EMT's and a nurse rushed my gurney through the emergency room.

Now I was on a cold metal table beneath glaring lights. A tiny body lay lifeless on my stomach. People in masks and green gowns tried gently to remove the small form from my arms.

"Take it from her nurse," one of them ordered.

"No!" I shouted—

***

I lay inert in a hospital bed for a week then spent three months in a private sanatorium, wrists bandaged, after I tried to make a ghost of myself (it's impossible to do the job properly with a dull hospital knife). During this time, Eddie visited me once. I guess the cool and competent Beverly had him so busy all day and night, he couldn't find time to come again. I learned this for a fact when a process server, claiming to be my brother, came to my room two months into my confinement. After the man left, the damn laughter filled my dreams and every waking hour.

The day Pam brought me home, cartons were on the living room floor.

"Eddie, are you here?" I called when I opened the door.

There was no answer.

Pam followed me in. "Looks like he couldn't wait to get his things out of here."

I moved to the bedroom. One at time, I opened then slammed Eddie's dresser drawers. Each was empty.

"You knew this was coming," Pam said.

I dropped onto the bed, my face in my hands.

She touched my shoulder. "It'll be all right—"

"It won't!" I cried. "It never will again."

Laughter sneaked through the window, circled the room, and settled next to me. Low, hoarse, manic, it cackled in my ear.

The apartment door opened. Footsteps came down the hall, and stopped at the bedroom door. "You're… here," Eddie stated the obvious.

"You couldn't get your stuff out before she came home?" Pam snarled.

"I… um… just a few more things, and I'll be gone."

"What happened to us, Eddie?" I said.

Aaahahahaaa, the ghost answered.

My soon-to-be ex turned away.

Pam stroked my face. "I'll be right back."

"Where are you going?" I asked.

"Just want to move my car to a proper parking spot."

When she left, I gathered my emotions and went to the living room. Eddie was leaning through the window.

"Hey, you little bastards, stay away from my stuff!" he hollered.

I moved to window, stood next to him. Eddie's car was parked two buildings away, the trunk open. Two kids fingered the cartons in it. Pam glanced up at the window, then crossed the street to shoo the kids away.

Aaahahahahahaaa.

I closed my eyes, grabbed my ears.

Eddie yelped.

My eyes shot open. I saw him lean further out the window. I saw his feet rise from the floor. He grabbed for the sill.

Aahahahaha.

His hand slipped. He screamed.

Pam raced to the broken body on the pavement.

***

"I didn't do it," I tell the court-appointed shrink. "Didn't push my husband out the window."

"But, only you and he were in the apartment," he says.

I sit back, arms wrapped around my chest. The prison blouse is rough to the touch. "It wasn't me."

"Who then, the ghost you insist haunts you? Your husband was a good six feet from the building—too far out to have just fallen."

I shrug.

"Mrs. Marks, I can't help if you aren't honest with me."

I *am* being honest, I want to say. But, why bother? This stranger in an expensive suit and polka dot bowtie won't believe me. Why would he? Pam doesn't, nor does Ken. They don't hear the constant laughter.

The man runs long, thin fingers through his graying hair then begins to gather pages from the table. "There's nothing more I can do here. I'll send my report to the judge in a week or so." He glances up, nods.

A matron unlocks the door. In three longs strides, she crosses the room, and takes my elbow. As she leads me to the barred door, I hear the shrink mutter, "Insanity defenses…" When I turn back, he's shaking his head.

The matron grabs my arm tighter.

I'm not insane! I want to shout at him. I open my mouth, but all that comes out is a long, manic *Aaahahahahaaa.*

The Holmes Society

Four twenty-something budding writers of mysteries have formed a group to examine old, unsolved crimes, and perhaps write about them. Their method: the logic of their favorite detective, Sherlock Holmes. This night, though, they have a real and present crime to solve: Judith James, one of the four, has received five anonymous threatening notes. As they work their way through this real-life mystery, Judith comes face-to-face with a horrendous crime she witnessed fifteen years before.

Memories are pesky children. You think they're tucked into bed, but just when you settle down for a quiet evening with friends, they wake, cry out, demand attention. This happened with Judith James, a witness to a scene so horrendous it needed forgetting.

Fifteen years ago Judith climbed from a school bus and rode the elevator the sixth floor of an apartment building on Park Avenue. She shrugged the backpack from her shoulders and dug in it for the key. The apartment door creaked open—her father still hadn't phoned the super to oil it. Inside all was silent.

"Mom," she called. "You home?"

She received no reply.

The child dropped her bag and coat on the kitchen table, and started down the dark hall. Her mother, a writer of mystery novels, would work in the den while Judith was in school. Often she became so engrossed in a plot, she didn't notice when her daughter arrived. At such times, Judith calling for her would fail to interrupt a conversation the writer might be having with characters in a new story.

"Mom," Judith whispered as she quietly pushed at the den door.

She expected her mother to wave her away; tell her, "Fix a snack, honey. I'll be there as soon as I finish this chapter."

When Judith peered through the door, the den seemed as it always was: bookshelves along two walls, two desks—her mother's and her father's. Photographs she'd known since the first time she was allowed in this room hung where they should be. One picture was of her sitting on Mom's lap with Daddy behind them, another was of Uncle Paul and Aunt Edith at their wedding. In a third, the five of them were together at the Central Park zoo. On the wall near his desk, Daddy grinned in a photograph taken the day he received the Pulitzer Prize. Judith didn't know what kind of prize Mr. Pulitzer handed out, but understood it was important—Daddy talked about it all the time. His prizewinning newspaper article was framed beneath his photo.

Still in the hall, hesitant to enter, Judith continued to scan the room. Her mother's chair was unoccupied. In the chair at the other desk—

"Daddy?"

He didn't answer, seemed to be asleep. This was not surprising. Her father was a reporter for the *Post*. Often out late chasing a story, when he was home he might fall asleep anywhere: the living room while he watched television; once even at the dinner table. Never in the den, though.

She tiptoed in. Then her eyes shot open wide.

Old Mrs. Shaunessy from next door heard the child scream—the walls of Manhattan apartments can be quite thin—and rushed over. It was she who telephoned 9-1-1.

***

The two uniform cops that were first on the scene saw Mrs. Shaunessy, her face ghost-white, sitting in the kitchen with a bawling Judith wrapped in her arms. The old woman, unable to speak, pointed down the hall. One cop remained in the kitchen while the other peeked into the den. When he returned a moment later, he said, "Gotta call the squad, get detectives and Crime Scene over here."

The elderly woman nodded, but didn't move.

Judith let out a wail.

Within fifteen minutes the apartment was filled with blue uniforms and rumpled suits. They found a woman's body sprawled on the floor near the damask window curtains, a small puddle of blood next to her head. Steam from the old radiator blew gentle ripples in her black hair. A man slumped in a desk chair had a red dot on his left temple. A twenty-two caliber pistol lay on the floor below his left hand. On the desk was a three volume of set of Sherlock Holmes stories. Next to this was a typed note, short, unsigned. Clipped to legal papers in which one James was the Plaintiff and another James the Respondent, it said, *I can't let you do this.*

The lead detective walked quietly on rubber-soled shoes from the den to the kitchen. "Either of them know what happened?" he asked.

The policewoman standing next to Judith and Mrs. Shaunessy said, "The woman here heard arguing earlier today. Can't get anything from the child."

At that moment, a well-dressed man of average height walked through the apartment door. He removed the hat covering his brown hair neatly parted on left, and took a step toward the den. "What's going on?" he demanded.

Judith shouted the first words she'd spoken since she'd screamed. "Uncle Paul!" She rushed to the man, and buried her face in the folds of his overcoat.

The detective stepped in front of the man. "Who are you?"

The man leaned to look past the detective.

"Uncle Paul..." Judith said, her voice gurgling with tears.

"I'm... uh, Paul James. Where's my brother, Ed? My sister-in-law? They'll tell you who I am."

"They're not available," the detective said. "Why are you here?"

Uncle Paul glanced around. "I... I work at Gracie Mansion... on the mayor's staff."

The detective unwound Judith's arms from her uncle's waist. "See to her," he told the policewoman, and led Paul to the den.

At the den door, Paul's hand went to his mouth. From the kitchen Judith heard him say, "That's Edward. And... and Elisa. Oh, lord. I... was in the neighborhood—a shop near Rockefeller Center. Suits on sale half off."

Twisting the brim of his hat, he stepped back from the den. "Needed a new suit for the City Hall Christmas party."

There were a number of questions the detective might have asked Judith's uncle: was his brother was left-handed; were Edward and Elisa James getting divorced? There was no need for such questions, though. To him, what happened was clear. The legal papers, the note, Mrs. Shaunessy's statement that she'd heard fierce arguing—a man's voice and a woman's—just when she'd sat down to lunch. The detective had no time to waste on the obvious. He had other, more urgent cases to deal with: a double homicide in Needle Park, a string of vicious push-in robberies on the Upper East Side.

In the hall, trembling, her face again buried in the folds of Uncle Paul's overcoat, Judith heard the detective complain to a uniform, "Guy's wife serves him with divorce papers outta the blue, it's a sure thing he's goin' after her."

"I would, *my* wife did me that way." The uniform agreed.

The detective crossed the room, pulled the curtains apart, and stared out the window at bare tree branches in Central Park. "Muggings every day out there," he muttered, "I should be chasin' down criminals instead of foolin' around with somethin' so simple a kid could write it up."

But, this wasn't what it appeared—though only ten years-old, Judith knew it wasn't. She tore away from her uncle, and dashed into the den.

"Daddy didn't!" she shouted. "He would never hurt me or Mom." She broke into tears and sank to the floor next to her mother.

The crime scene tech, white haired and badly in need of a shave, glanced up from the body. "Get this kid out of here," he hissed. "Jeez, what wrong with you people?"

The detective flushed. A burly cop grabbed Judith around the waist and hauled her, kicking and crying from the den. He handed her to Uncle Paul, who dragged her from the apartment.

The sight and the details of the carnage, the voice of the detective saying, "Simple case, guy killed the wife, then himself," should have stayed front and center in the child's mind. It didn't. The mind protects itself. As a jungle does, Judith's mind quickly overgrew with leafy vines behind which those pesky memories took refuge.

***

On an evening like many others, Judith James, now twenty-five with curls as long and black as her mother's had been, carried a tray of cheese and crackers from the kitchen of her third-floor Greenwich Village walk-up, to her modest living room. Reminiscent of her parents' den, the room had a floor-to-ceiling bookshelves filled with mystery novels and criminology texts. Three large volumes, *The Complete Cases of Sherlock Holmes*, were stacked on the scarred lamp table next to her sofa, ready for reference if the need arose. It was just past eight o'clock. Sirens whined down Seventh Avenue. *Crime City*, Judith had called Manhattan since that night fifteen years ago. Perhaps this is why she chose to write about it—as her mother had in her way; as her father had in his. Not that she remembered much about her parents—blocking out the scene of their death had also blocked the memories of everything before. So, except for the framed photographs on the wall near the bookcase, she knew only what Uncle Paul and Aunt Edith had told her over the years.

She glanced at the picture of her aunt and uncle as she entered the room, then at the diploma hung just above it. The Latin said she was a Master of Fine Arts. Uncle Paul had made sure Judith received a proper education—he and Aunt Edith had raised her, treated her as though she were their own child. Also on the wall were the picture of her father and the framed copy of his Pulitzer Prize article.

As Judith arranged the snack tray on the table in front of the brown corduroy sofa she'd found in an East Village second-hand shop, she was startled by pounding on her door. She grabbed the rounded armrest of the sofa, and her head swung in that direction.

Again the fist pounded, and now the rapping was accompanied by a call in a British accent—clearly put-on, since the voice had a nasal Brooklyn undertone: "Wake up, Watson, wake up. The game's afoot."

An alto giggle surrounded the voice.

"Coming." Judith released a breath she hadn't realized she'd been holding. Her eyes fell on the crumpled note next to the cheese platter. It was this note that had her on edge. She hoped the friends she'd made in her mystery writing group could help her past her fear. But, were the voices outside her door really those of her friends? She couldn't be certain of anything these days. On her toes, with one hazel eye closed, she peered through the peephole. At last satisfied, she drew the chain and unlatched the apartment door.

"I'm so glad you're here, Ira," she said to the tall, painfully thin young man with a prominent Adam's apple and a meerschaum pipe clutched between his teeth.

"Not Ira, Watson." He pointed to the deerstalker cap he wore. "I'm Sherlock."

"Uh-huh," she said. "And I'm not Judy, I'm Professor Moriarity." For the first time since she'd returned from work she felt at ease.

"In that case," said the other young man who now filled her doorway, "you're under arrest."

He was shorter than Ira, and had a long nose and close-cropped hair. His navy Police Department tee-shirt emphasized his well-muscled chest when he pulled plastic handcuffs—a child's toy—from his back pocket.

"You tell her, Lestrade," said the young woman who followed him inside.

She was dressed in green hospital scrubs, and her red hair bounced with each step. A student nurse, Angela Walker had just come off shift at Columbia General. She glanced at the handcuffs, and her brown almond-shaped eyes lit. "*Hmm*, this could get kinky."

The young man who'd called himself Lestrade wasn't Conan Doyle's Scotland Yard Inspector, but he *was* a cop, the third generation of McNamaras to pin on New York City's badge. Richard hadn't the dedication his forebears showed toward the job, though. At least, not to chasing criminals on foot. A budding writer, he desired to nab crooks on paper. This was how he'd met Judith, Ira Statten, and the red-headed Angela, and why he gathered with them several nights each month to construct puzzles which might have stymied their fictitious hero. As it turned out, Richard McNamara was the link the group needed. He brought them unsolved crimes, cold cases his precinct's detectives spoke about. He, Ira, Angela, and Judith used these cased to test their Holmesean logic.

Picking at a sleeve of her loose green blouse, Judith sighed. "Must we go through this every time we get together?"

Ira pinched her cheek. "Of course we must." He plopped down on the sofa, and stuffed a chunk of cheese into his mouth. "Stilton," he said while chewing. "A perfect complement to crime."

Angela shook her head. To Judith, she said, "With these manners, he might be Holmes reincarnated." Daintily, she slid onto the sofa next to him, tilted the box of wine, and poured two glasses.

Judith shot a look at her. She settled on the other side of Ira, and took the drink from his hand.

"Uh, yes…" Ira cleared his throat.

Angela smirked.

Richard laughed. "Ah, the Woman—seems we've settled into our roles."

Grinning, Angela leaned toward Ira. She seemed pleased with the idea of playing Irene Adler, the only woman able to touch Holmes's heart.

Ira slid forward and dropped his cap on the table. As he did, he noticed the note. "Another one?"

Judith chewed her lower lip.

"When did it come?" Richard reached for the note.

"What's it say?" Angela's playfulness was gone.

"It was under my door when I got home."

"Read it," Ira said. He leaned back with his lips pursed.

Richard read: "YOU MUST STOP. NO MORE WARNINGS!" He turned the page over, examined the other side, then passed the note.

"The words seem to be cut from some magazine," Ira said.

Angela grabbed the note from Ira's hand. "Uh-uh. It's from an old *Newport News* Catalogue. I recognize it— my mother gets them. Great clothes in those catalogues— and prices even you could afford, Judy."

"Doesn't matter where it comes from." Richard gulped a large swallow of his wine. "This has gotten way out of hand. We've gotta take this note to the precinct, get the department involved."

Judith curled her legs under her, and leaned into a corner of the sofa. "I tried when I got the last one. I'm not a complete idiot."

"If you say so," Angela muttered.

Ira smacked the redhead's arm.

"What?" She glanced at Ira from the corner of her eyes. "I was just joking."

"This isn't a laughing matter," Richard said. "These threats—it's way more than we can handle."

What do you suggest, then?" Judith's stomach churned. Her hand shaking, she leaned to the table, reaching for her wineglass. "The police aren't going to help. The desk sergeant I spoke to said he'd give the note to a detective. It's more than two weeks, and I haven't heard from anyone."

Ira rubbed his forehead. "Which leaves?"

Turning to her bookcase, Judith's eyes roamed from the criminology texts to her mother's mystery novels, then settled on the volumes of Sherlock Holmes stories on her lamp table. At last she said, "That leaves us."

Ira's eyes went wide and Richard shook his head. "What?" they said in unison.

Angela sighed. Richard stared out the window. Ira swallowed a breath. This wasn't an anonymous cold case to which they might imagine solutions. This was real. It was happening to someone they knew!

Judith slouched back. "I... it's the only thing I can think of to do."

"But—"

"No, don't you see? The police won't get involved until somebody's killed." Her mind shot back to her parents' death—their murder, it didn't matter what Uncle Paul insisted. "If you don't want to attend my funeral," she said, "we *have* to figure this out."

Six eyes turned to Ira.

Sucking on his meerschaum, he said, "She's right."

Angela's glossed lips turned up in a cat-like grin.

"Where do we start?" Richard said. "We don't know what this is about."

"Start at the beginning," Judith said. "That's what Aunt Edith used to tell me when I had to write a school essay."

"Yes. It's the same thing with writing a story," Ira agreed. "Writing a mystery novel is why we got together in the first place." He settled back with a look of determination. "We can do this—it could even be a better story than the one we've been working on."

Angela's heavily mascaraed eyelashes jumped up and down. She snuggled against Ira's shoulder.

Richard frowned at the flirtatious display. "Tighten your chastity belt," he said to the redhead. "If we're gonna do this, there can't be any distractions. Which means," he went on before she could take umbrage, "No making like a bug trying to crawl into Ira's bed."

Angela's face turned the color of her hair. She clenched her fists.

"He's right." Judith leaned forward, glaring.

Her eyes now slyly examining the room, Angela looked to be more cat than bug.

Ira nodded. "No distractions. We've gotta figure out who's sending Judy these threats. And we've gotta do it before she gets hurt."

The grin still on her lips, Angela rested her head on the back of the brown sofa. Richard sat up straight in the armchair.

"Think back, Judy," Ira said. "When did you get the first threat?"

She glanced at the photo of Aunt Edith and Uncle Paul. All these years while she tried so hard to recall some small detail she'd seen the day her parents died—the smallest thing which would explain what happened in their den—her aunt encouraged her to sit quietly, breathe deeply, not fight the memory. Given time, Aunt Edith had patiently instructed, the memory would return on its own. Fifteen years, though, and the memory still hadn't returned. Maybe Uncle Paul was right: she was better off not remembering.

"Still with us, Judy?" Ira asked.

His rather high-pitched voice yanked her mind back to her small apartment with its unmatched furnishings, and to what seemed be a threat to her life.

"I… I think it must have been a year ago. Almost a year. Yes, that's right. I remember. It was a few days after I had dinner with my aunt and uncle. While we cleaned up afterward, I told Aunt Edith we'd started this group."

"Good. Good. Now, what was happening back then?"

"Happening?"

"Yeah, you know," Angela said. "Did you break up with someone you were sleeping with?" She eyed Ira suggestively.

"Give it a rest, Angie, would you?" Richard said with more than a hint of annoyance in his voice and on his face.

"What? I'm just trying to help."

"Yeah, and some kind of help is the kind—"

"Knock it off, both of you." Ira smacked his wine glass on the coffee table. "We'll never solve this if you're gonna fight."

Sulking, Angela pulled away from him. "I wasn't fighting. If she had a messy breakup, it could be why she's getting threats."

"Okay, I see your point," Ira conceded, and refilled his glass from the box of wine. "Did you, Judy?"

"Uh-uh. I haven't seen anyone seriously for a couple of years." Not that she hadn't wanted to. Ira just didn't seemed interested. Her eyes turned to the photograph of her father.

At this moment, one of those pesky memories poked its nose out from behind some trees in her mental jungle. *Interested* echoed in her mind. A conversation overhead: her father on the phone, angry at someone. She closed her eyes, and gave the memory permission to speak.

The door to her parents den had been open a crack. She was in the hall.

"I'm not interested in hearing excuses," her father had said to the telephone. "You're the one who screwed up your marriage." After a short pause, he said, "I don't give a damn who you are—"

His raised voice startled her. She stepped back.

Daddy must have heard the floor creak. He pulled the door open, and shouted, "Go to your room, Judy!" Then he slammed the door.

"What is it?" Ira took the pipe from his mouth and laid it on the table. "Did you remember something?"

She yanked back her black hair. "Uh-uh. No." She lifted the note from the table. "At… at least, not about this."

Ira reached for the note, and again inspected it. "Tell us. As Holmes used to say, nothing's unimportant. Not the smallest detail."

Her almond-shaped eyes glowing, Angela smiled at him.

"It really has nothing to do with—" Bile burned in Judith's stomach. "It's something from long ago." She narrowed her eyes, as if trying to peer into the past. After a moment, she moaned, "I can't remember."

Richard leaned from his armchair, and took her hand. "It's okay. It'll come to you in time."

Warmth spread upward from her hand. His touch, his words, brought back memories of the affection Aunt Edith showered on her.

"Let's get back to the note," Angela said curtly. "It could be a coded message."

Ira's eyes swung to *The Complete Cases of Sherlock Holmes* on the scarred lamp table. "You mean like in *The Valley of Fear?*"

"Why not?" Angela appeared pleased to have led them in this direction.

"Maybe," Richard said. "Let me take a closer look." He released Judith's hand, and pulled a magnifying glass from the pocket of his jeans. "See here—these squiggly lines? It's kind of like—"

"Let me see." Ira snatched the page and the magnifying glass. "Yes, yes. Like in *The Adventure of the Dancing Men!*"

Judith stared past the window blinds at a streetlight flickering on Seventh Avenue. *Squiggly lines*, she thought. *Lines...* She'd heard her father say that, too.

"Those white lines you're chasing after," he'd yelled into the phone. *"I'm putting an end to them. The* Post *is running my follow-up story on Saturday. After that, the police—"*

His words became blurred when she closed her bedroom door.

"See the arrows pointing from one letter to another?" Ira's finger traced the arrows. He took a pen from his shirt pocket, and scribbled on the bottom of the page. "If I arrange the letters this way, it says—" He caught his breath.

"What?" Richard asked.

Ira held up the sheet.

"Omigod!" Angela pulled the page from his hand. "It says IRA STOP!" Her expression didn't quite match the shock in her voice. "Now they're after you."

"The more I think about those arrows, the less sense a code makes," Richard said. "Too many letters are left over."

Angela glared at him. A small growl escaped from her throat. As if to force their investigation back in the direction she chose, she said, "Judy, what do you make of this?"

"Huh?"

"Where's your mind?" Angela smoothed the blouse of her hospital scrubs. "We're trying to help you, and now Ira's in trouble!"

Richard shook his head. "No, this makes no sense. It's like someone's hiding inside the puzzle, taunting us. Let me see the page again. Uh-huh—see this? I can make these letters say almost anything. Look: I take *A-N-G-I* from *warning*, add the *E* from *more*, and now the note's talking to you, Angie—that's what people call you isn't it? So, who were *you* sleeping with?"

Her frown pulled her carefully plucked eyebrows down in a stiff *V*. She clearly was not at all pleased by the question.

"Stick your lip back in," Richard said, "Not everything's about you. Although... I wonder—" He glanced at Angela.

Ira looked hard at him. "Wonder what?"

Richard shook his head. "I need to think."

Brushing an invisible crumb from her blouse, Angela said, "You're probably right: Judy's causing this problem. Didn't you once tell us your father got his Pulitzer Prize for an exposé of a drug ring working out of City Hall? Maybe that's what this is about."

"Could it be?" Ira asked, more at ease now that it appeared he might not be the target of the threatening note.

"I... I don't— No, I can't see how. The people Dad wrote about were convicted."

"But, are they still in jail?" Angela reached for the cheese knife, sliced a chunk of Stilton, and balanced it on a cracker."

"If they're out, maybe they're after revenge," Ira said.

"On me? Whatever for?"

Richard again took Judith's hand, and looked into hazel eyes which were now wide as tears formed. "Is it possible the drug ring went higher in the mayor's administration than anyone knew?"

"How would I—?"

"Think carefully. Did your father leave you anything—documents, notes from his story?"

"I—"

Richard squeezed her hand. Urgency in his voice, he said, "Picture your father's den as it was the day you found your parents."

Judith's tears spilled down her cheeks. "I can't."

"Try!"

"Yes, yes! When you eliminate everything possible—" Ira leaned forward, urging her the way Holmes might have.

"Yeah, we know," Richard said. "Let the girl think, would you!"

Just as Judith opened her mouth to moan again about an inability to recall what happened when she was ten, there was a loud knock on the door.

Angela jumped. Richard gasped.

Her body and voice both trembling, Judith cried, "They're here!" though she had no idea who *they* might be.

Only Ira remained calm. "It's the pizza delivery boy."

"How do you know it's not whoever's threatening me?" Judith pulled at her black hair. "Don't open the door!"

Ira lifted his meerschaum from the table, and again sucked on it. As calmly as Sherlock Holmes might have explained how he knew a client had just returned from India, he said, "First of all, I smell the pepperoni. Second, the boy who makes the deliveries from the shop on the corner walks with a decided limp—didn't you hear it as he climbed the stairs? Third, I called for the pie just before we got here. They said it would take about an hour." He examined his watch. "I see it's right on time."

He rose from the sofa, strolled to the door, and opened it without checking the peephole.

"Judy James here?" The voice was rough, and cracked as it rose. This might have been the sound of a street hood.

Judith groaned. Her body limp, she slid from the sofa into Richard's arms.

"Hope you don't mind, Judy?" Ira said. "I ordered the pie in your name. Anyone have a few bucks? I'm a little short this week."

Still holding tight to Judith, Richard snarled, "What's wrong with you, Ira? You nearly frightened the life from this poor girl!"

"I don't see why," he responded as Angela slipped two ten dollar bills into his hand. "I told you it was the pizza I ordered." He sounded truly surprised. After all, if Sherlock Holmes announced a pizza was at the door, no one would have questioned *him*.

***

They munched their meal in silence—or, rather, three of them munched. Judith refused to look at the pie. The abject fear she'd felt when Ira opened the door had made a tight braid of her digestive tract. So she sat, eyes locked on the window, her mind completely absorbed by the manner in which her lace curtains fluttered when the radiator kicked on. The sound was same as the radiators made in the apartment the day she found her parents.

After half an hour, Ira belched and closed the lid of the pizza box. As if the conversation were continuing without a gap, he said, "*Is* it possible these threats are because of the drug ring your father uncovered?"

Richard gathered the residue of the pizza, and started for the kitchen. As he reached the door, he turned back. "Could your father have left a clue for you?"

Judith twisted the hem of her green silk blouse. "For me? I was only ten. What kind of clue would he have thought I'd understand?"

The kitchen garbage can opened then clattered closed. Richard leaned through the door. "Did you ever look through his things?"

"Even if I'd thought to, I couldn't." Judith tipped the wine box to her glass, hoping another drink might calm her tingling nerves. "Uncle Paul closed up my parents' apartment. He sold everything so he could pay for my college and grad school. Besides their photographs, all I have are those Sherlock Holmes books." She thought for a few seconds. "Those were on my father's desk!"

Ira's head swiveled to the lamp table, and he jumped for the thick volumes. One-by-one, he turned them upside down and shook the pages. Nothing slid out.

"The book jackets!" Angela shouted. "Maybe there really is a mystery in all this nonsense." Clearly excited by the prospect of a hidden clue from a long-ago crime, she dropped the idea of a code spelled out by the letters of the threatening note. "Check the jackets!" She lifted one of the books and ripped the dust cover from it.

Ira leaned over, looking at the paper in her hands. "Anything?" he asked.

She shook her head.

Judith gaped at the torn shreds of the book jacket strewn at Angela's feet. "That..." She sniffed, and her voice quivered. "It was all I had of my parents."

On his knees gathering the torn dust cover, Richard glanced over his well-muscled shoulder at the student nurse. "You're an idiot, Angela." Looking up at Ira, he added, "If I get mugged and I'm lying on the street outside Columbia General, remind me to die before I let this idiot examine me."

Sneering, Angela said, "I just might let you die."

Richard growled and jumped to his feet. His hand bent as if it were a claw, he reached for the student nurse.

With a motion almost faster than the eye, Ira grabbed the outstretched arm. "What's done is done," he said. "Let it go."

Richard wasn't about to let it go. His face red, he returned to the thought which struck him just before the pizza arrived. "Where were you this afternoon, Angela?"

"What do you mean, where was I?"

"Just what I said: where were you?"

"I don't have to tell you—you're not my mother." Her face was now also red.

Ira released Richard's arm. "What are you getting at?"

"I think our so-called friend over here has been sliding the notes under Judy's door."

"You can't mean that." Ira's Adams apple bobbed more than it usually did.

"Oh, but I do." Taking a deep breath, Richard returned to his chair in front of the bookshelves. "She had a late shift today." He picked up the note from the coffee table. "That means she had time to deliver this before she went uptown. I'll bet if we check the hospital's personnel records, we'd find the same was true each of the five times Judy got one of these threats."

Ira's brow furrowed so deeply it looked as though a plow had run across his forehead.

Her face a deeper crimson, the redhead's eyes flashed from one member of the group to another.

"Angela?" Ira said.

"I... I didn't." She turned to Richard. Anger flaring, she said, "And you can't prove I did."

"Maybe not in a court I can't, but among us— And there's more. When most people explain what they've seen or done, they just state the facts: I was here; I did this or that; I overheard this other thing. But, a liar—even the best of them can't help but embellish." He stared deep into Angela's eyes. "It's a psychological need to sell her story."

"The lie's in the details," Ira agreed.

Richard nodded. "That's what Holmes said—the more a story's filled with detail, the greater the chance it's a fabrication."

"Sherlock Holmes never said anything of the kind." Angela lifted one of the Holmes books, and held it out. "Show me where he said that!"

They ignored her.

"Yes," Judith said. "It's like when I made up an excuse for why I didn't want to come home from college to have Thanksgiving with Aunt Edith and Uncle Paul. I told my aunt the flight times and the distance I was from the airport. I even named each of the texts I had to read from over the holiday weekend."

"Exactly." Richard sat back with his hands splayed on the armrests. "Now, remember what Angela told us about this last note?" He turned to her. "You couldn't leave it at the letters were cut from some magazine. No. You were specific about what catalog they came from—even suggested Judy could afford the clothes in the catalog."

Tears filled Judith's eyes. "But why, Angela? Why? I thought you're my friend."

The redhead shimmied into a corner of the brown corduroy sofa, and her eyes flicked between Judith and the apartment door. "It's this dumb club of yours," she blurted. "Always Sherlock Holmes said this and Sherlock Holmes said that. And the way you treat Judy like she's the be-all and end-all—like my mother treated my sister." She jumped from the sofa. "I've just had it with—" She snatched the note from the table, tore it in half, and tore it again. "You wanted a mystery, so I gave you one!" She grabbed her coat. At the door, she shouted, "You should be thanking me!"

As the door slammed, Judith said, "Why'd she do this to me? I don't get it."

"No," Richard said, "she's the one who doesn't get it."

In the silence following the storm of Angela's departure, Ira asked, "Did Holmes really say that?"

"Say what?" Richard said.

"The thing about a liar's embellishment."

The young cop smiled, and shrugged.

Ira patted his arm. "Good bluff, Lestrad."

Richard bowed his head.

"Oh, well." Ira reached for his deerstalker. "I guess this is the end of The Holmes Society."

"Doesn't have to be. There are still three of us, and dozens of cold cases in the precinct's files. We don't need

Angie to solve them. I'll get my hands on one for when we meet next week." He rose to leave. "What do say, Judy—you still want to do this?"

Since Angela's outburst, Judith had been standing at her window, staring out.

Richard touched her shoulder. "You okay?"

She didn't respond.

Ira laid his hand on her other shoulder. "Hey, don't let that redheaded witch get to you. The threats are over now. Be glad they weren't serious."

She turned to them with tears in her eyes. Richard's bluff had awakened another memory. It stared up from the torn dust covers of the Sherlock Holmes books, and whispered her name. Those books were next to the divorce papers. But, it wasn't her parents' marriage which was breaking up—she was now more certain than she'd ever been. Something overheard, Richard had said earlier. Yes. But, this time the voice speaking to her wasn't her father's. It was a woman's, her words clipped, harsh, saying, "We're together because of the child—don't ever forget that!" It wasn't her mother who spoke. Elisa James's voice was always calm, even when she was angry. Her father used to be amused by such cool control. "I don't know how you do it, Lissy," he would say. "If the world were ending, you'd spend the day cleaning up so God wouldn't think you kept a messy house." No. it wasn't her mother's voice she recalled, it was Aunt Edith's. Which meant—

"What is it?" Ira's grip tightened on her shoulder.

She didn't hear him or feel his hand. "That means," she mumbled. "No! It can't be—"

"What can't be?" Richard wrapped an arm around her waist.

Her eyes opened wider. What was it Richard had said? Embellishment? Another thing overheard: *Rockefeller Center. A men's shop. Suits on sale half-off.* The words hadn't meant anything at the time. She'd hardly heard what he said. He was with her, his strong arms comforting her. The detective, so annoyed at being forced to take notes at what he'd called a simple murder-suicide, hadn't reacted, either.

Panting now, Judith struggled for air.

Richard held her tighter. "You're worrying me."

"It can't be." She began to tremble. "He couldn't."

"Who couldn't do what?"

"Call Angela's cellphone," Richard said, "Get her back here! Maybe she has a sedative of some kind."

"Help me get her to the sofa." Ira's gentle touch on her wrist urged Judith away from the window.

Settled on the sofa with Richard on one side and Ira on the other, Judith grasped a volume of the Holmes set, and clutched it against her chest. "He never asked," she said. "He never—"

Ira took his cellphone from his shirt pocket and punched in numbers.

Richard pulled Judith to his side and held her. "Who didn't ask?"

"Who?" she repeated as if she had no idea she was in Richard's arms.

"Who?" he said again. "Judy, come back to me—" He glanced at Ira "—to us."

"Yes, we're still at Judy's place," Ira said into his phone. "Get your ass back here! We need you—"

"What are you talking about, Judy," Richard said.

"—No, not later," Ira shouted to his phone. "Now!"

Oblivious to the concern surrounding her, Judith continued to moan. "He never asked. My uncle lived on the Upper East Side of Manhattan, he worked at City Hall. What... how... why..."

"What's going on, Judy." Richard stroked her shoulder, then her face.

She knew the *why*, of course. It had been there all along, hanging on her wall beneath her father's picture.

Daddy *had* left her a clue. Now the clue called to her, and her heart broke. It had taken years for her to learn to trust again. As if it were a wine glass thrown against her apartment wall, her trust was shattered. "No one ever asked," she groaned.

"What?" Ira and Richard said as one.

As Richard brushed her tears away with his thumb, a fist pounded on the door. When Ira opened it, Angela rushed in. "What the hell's going on? Why'd you call me?"

Ira pointed at Judith. "She's remembered something."

"What?"

"We don't know. She isn't able to tell us."

Although Judith now knew, what could she do? Her aunt and uncle had raised her. For fifteen years, she'd been their child—

Angela took Judith's hands. The anger which had filled the apartment ten minutes earlier forgotten, she whispered, "Breath slowly. That's right: inhale, hold the breath, exhale."

As Judith's breathing became more relaxed, the book fell from her grasp. The sound as it clattered on the cheese tray seemed to bring her back from the jungle of her past. She glanced at her three friends, seeing their worried expressions. "I don't know what to do," she said.

It took a while to get the story from Judith. Between groans and moans, and enough tears to empty a tissue box, she relived the scene of her parents' murder. It all fit into place now. Her father had been yelling at Uncle Paul on the phone. Uncle Paul's and Aunt Edith's names must have been those on the divorce papers the detective never examined. Uncle Paul worked at City Hall. He must have been the subject of the follow-up article her father wrote— the article which wasn't published because it was never found. It must have been Uncle Paul Mrs. Shaunessy heard arguing with her mother that day.

"He raised me," Judith said when she at last finished. "He and Aunt Edith did. I was their daughter." Again she broke into tears. "How can I tell the police I think my uncle murdered my mother and father?"

They were silent for a long while, Ira at the window staring down Seventh Avenue, Angela sipping at the dregs of the boxed wine, Richard holding Judith while she whimpered. At last Ira said, "I wonder if this is how Holmes would have felt if he learned his brother, Mycroft, was a murderer."

Angela swallowed the last of her wine. "It doesn't matter. There's no evidence."

Richard released Judith, and leaned back on the sofa. "Maybe not. But, what Judy remembers might be enough to get a bright young cop to quietly look into the case—those divorce papers must be in the file."

"Accusing my uncle—how can I do that to Aunt Edith?"

Again they fell silent.

After a minute, Richard said, "The choice sure isn't easy."

Still staring down the Avenue, Ira said, "It's not as hard as all that. What would Holmes have done?"

***

The condominium of Paul and Edith James took up half the sixth floor of the building straddling Seventieth Street and Third Avenue. Bent at the waist, Judith sat at the edge of the large sectional sofa, her hands clasped between her legs. On her right, Ira lounged back with his hand on her shoulder. Angela sat on her left, an oversized shoulder bag clutched on her lap. Aunt Edith, tall, blond, and perfectly made up even at eight in the morning, leaned against the antique Venetian lady's writing desk, her fingers spread on the marble top. Uncle Paul was not present—an hour ago, two detectives had invited him for a conversation at

Manhattan's Midtown North Precinct. Wanting to hear the confession dragged from Paul James, Richard had accompanied the detectives.

Last week, as the clock in Judith's apartment neared midnight, Richard had said, "I don't care much what Holmes would have done in this situation, I know what *I've* gotta do."

"Don't! No. I can't let you—" Judith was so hoarse, she struggled to get the words out. "I... I... No! Oh, god, oh, god, why? How can I—? I can't!"

She hated the man she now was sure had murdered her father and mother. She adored the man who'd bought her cotton candy at the circus each year, who'd taken her to Central Park to ride the camel, who'd gone to her school's PTA meetings.

"Was it your uncle or your aunt who did those things," Angela had asked.

"I... Oh, god, I can't remember. I... can't think!"

Richard headed for the door.

Don't!" Judith cried to him.

She wasn't heard. His footsteps already thumped on the second floor landing. Perhaps he was at last becoming a cop the McNamara family could be proud of. The next morning he dug the James file from the precinct's basement Cold Case storage, and carried it up two flights to the Detective Bureau. It took an entire day to convince the sergeant to look at it.

Judith hadn't stopped crying during the entire next week. This morning Richard had telephoned, and now as she sat before her aunt, she broke into sobs. She'd betrayed this woman, taken her husband from her. Her lips trembling, struggling for words, Judith's head swiveled from the ornate faux fireplace, to the archway and the apartment's dining room beyond. What could she say? How would she ever be forgiven? She'd lost another family. This time it was *her* fault.

At last, into the strained silence, Ira said to Edith James. "Your husband never should have given Judy that framed article her father wrote. Eventually it was bound to jog her memory."

Aunt Edith straightened up and gave a small, throaty laugh. "Paul didn't give her the article," she said. "I did." She took both of Judith's hands, pulled her gently from the sofa, and wrapped her in an embrace. Kissing her hair, she whispered, "I hoped you'd remember one day."

"You... knew all along?" Judith said.

Aunt Edith also was crying.

"Why didn't you tell me... do something about...?"

She held Judith out. "You were so young, needed so much care. I couldn't give you what you needed by myself. Since you knew in your heart your father hadn't—well, I wanted to wait until you were ready to accept what you had to do."

Angela grabbed Ira's arm. "Is this how Holmes would have ended this case?"

His eyes on Judith and Aunt Edith, he said, "I don't know, and right now I don't care. We did the right thing."

Niagara Falling

In his second year of college, Richard Morrow left Corrie Wilder, the girl down the block, behind when he fled what he saw as a crumbling Niagara Falls. He wanted, he told her, a glorious future in Manhattan. Corrie, though, loved her home town. Thirty years and several divorces later Richard has found the success he sought. He's the senior partner of a prestigious Manhattan law firm. But, there has been a cost: long days with the single focus of building his career has stiffened him; the women he married sought only the extravagant social lifestyle his contacts would bring. Now he receives a letter from Corrie, asking him for a favor. When he returns to Niagara Falls to help her for what he thinks will be but a few days, he wonders if might have found the happiness he really sought with the girl from down the block.

This was my memory of Corrie Wilder: hair the color of summer wheat growing on Heimlich's farm; skin as translucent as the Niagara River before it flows into the rapids; body as lithe as a beech tree seedling on Goat Island; a stubborn streak as difficult as Mrs. Maloney's twelfth grade calculus class.

Through high school and two years of college, we roamed the back roads of Western New York. Her curiosity drew us into the long abandoned, Nabisco silos where I saw crumbling limestone. She saw stairways to the moon. I stood, hands on hips, at the gates of plots where chemicals with exotic names were reputedly interred. She scaled the rusted, chain link fences to examine glowing stones. On streets picketed by *For Sale* signs, I saw ramshackle houses surrounded by roof slates fallen on lawns overgrown with weeds. She thrilled to the promise of new friends who might dwell there tomorrow. Though I saw no worth in the cracked bricks of our small city, she had plans for me. We would marry, she said, and grow old in this tumble-down town as our parents had.

"I've been accepted at NYU," I told her at the end of my sophomore year at Buffalo State. "They'll transfer most of my credits."

Midnight, the movie at the drive-in had ended an hour ago. Parked on a dirt lane off River Road, I gazed south over the dark stand of maples and white cedars guarding the river.

Corrie's contented smile turned downward. "Why?"

When I didn't respond, she grabbed my face and turned my head until I had no choice but to look at her. Her hazel eyes with shimmering brown flecks locked on mine.

"What's there you can't find here?" she asked.

"A future," I said.

"Your future's here with me." When I didn't respond, she shouted, "Richard Alan Morrow, you don't love me!"

I leaned against the car door, avoiding her touch. Love her? I was twenty. What did I know of love?

"I'll come back as soon as I graduate," I lied. Loving Corrie, marrying her, would be a snare. We lived in a place where sky-darkening smokestacks were now corpses, their flesh rotting, their souls reincarnated someplace else. I was an eaglet, born to soar beyond the ruins of yesterday's glory.

Tears stained her cheeks.

A car sputtered down the road. Its headlamps cast an eerie patina on the trees. When I raised my left hand to fight the glare, I recognized Hal Silvestri's Plymouth. He must have recognized my pickup, and the blare of his horn drove birds to flight. Then he was gone. As I would soon be.

"Two years and I'll be back," I said, so Corrie could hang on to her dream a while longer. "You'll see, two years isn't so long."

I left for Manhattan in the fall, returned on holidays and semester breaks the first year. The second year, I returned at Christmas. Then not at all. Five years later, I received an invitation to Corrie's wedding. I wasn't able to attend. New associates at the Wall Street law firm of Marcus & Cornwall had to put in nearly a hundred hours a week. I sent a gift, and a short note wishing her a wonderful life. If I felt a sense of loss, I was too busy to realize it.

***

Last April I sat behind my desk, my black Armani suit carefully pressed and my red, blue, and white power tie held in place by a gold initial pin. Just past ten my secretary brought me the morning mail, organized so I could quickly review the correspondence before she filed it with the cases

I was handling. At the bottom of the pile, I saw an envelope addressed to Richard Morrow, Esq., of Marcus, Cornwall & Morrow. The return address said it came from Mrs. Corrie Silvestri, Niagara Falls, NY.

The unopened letter in my hand, I swiveled in my chair until I faced the empty skyline where the World Trade Center once stood. While I flicked the edge of the envelope, I recalled the town in which I was born and the hazel-eyed girl I once knew. I'd thought of her at times over the past thirty years—when my first marriage failed, when the second one did. Now the senior partner of a prestigious firm, I'd found the success I craved in a big city. Would I have found happiness if I'd stayed at home with the girl from down the block?

"Is something wrong?" my secretary asked.

I bit my lip.

"You're scheduled for a conference on the Whitestone matter in ten minutes," she reminded me.

Outside the windowed wall of my office, a plane tilted its wings, and headed north.

As I tore open the envelope, I said, "Tell them I'll be a few minutes late."

I wonder if you remember me, Corrie's letter began. *I'm the girl who shoved you into Cheektowaga Creek.*

The smile I saw mirrored in the window was not as broad as the one I, a freckle-faced kid, had worn when I climbed from that creek and shook like a dog to spray her. Yet, it was the first true smile I'd managed in some time. Clients expect a stern visage from their attorney. It signals strength, determination. My life had been built on meeting client expectations.

The rest of the first page contained other memories. She didn't come to the point until halfway down page two. This was typical of the Corrie I'd known: it took her a while to get there—except when *there* was me, and she decided I'd be her husband. She'd informed me of that as quickly as the thought entered her mind. At the recollection, I laughed out loud, flipped the page, and read down the other side.

My husband passed last year, she wrote. *You might recall he was an artist, and rather successful—he painted what he felt about the town you grew up in—*

I tilted back in my chair, and again glanced through the window. I'd seen several of Hal's paintings when I attended a charity function at the Museum of Modern Art. For a moment, I felt a tinge of jealousy. Corrie had found contentment with a man whose work would last millennia. *What have I accomplished? Preservation of other peoples' wealth? Fifty years from now, what will that matter?*

I swiveled to my desk, and laid the letter on the blotter.

Hal's Will says he wants the bulk of his estate to start a foundation for the development of artists up here, so I'm writing to you. I know you've set this kind of thing up for others, and I thought maybe—

I glanced up. *She knows the branch of law I specialize in? Has she thought of me through the years?*

The intercom interrupted my musing. "Mister Morrow, everyone's in the conference room."

"Thank you, Jean," I said. "Tell them I'm on my way."

I folded the letter, and slipped it into my jacket pocket.

"Get me on a flight to Niagara Falls, would you?" I said to her, as I left my office.

One eyebrow raised, Jean glanced up from her computer screen. "When?"

I leaned over her desk. "What does my calendar look like?"

"You're booked solid tomorrow and Thursday." She pointed to the calendar page. "Friday's also full. You have a meeting on the Kushner estate, and—"

"Cancel those appointments," I called, as I rushed down the hall. "Get me on a flight."

***

I left my rental car in the Hilton lot. Dressed in a dark suit and tie, I strolled to Pine Avenue. It was as if my feet remembered these streets: every crack in the pavement, each pothole in the road. The hospital where I was born had grown, been given a face-lift. Asker's Ice Cream was no longer across the street, and Mr. Donut was now Frank's Donuts. Different name, same place. Shops lining the street were nothing like the stately stores on Manhattan's Upper East Side. At Portage Road, I passed the old Niagara Falls High School. A sign on the lawn declared it was now something called NACC—the Niagara Arts and Cultural Center. My pace slowed. The Five and Dime was gone from Nineteenth Street. As a child, I'd drooled over toys in the bins lining the walls.

I stopped and peered through the window of Como's, the Italian restaurant where my parents held my high school graduation party. An elderly waitress waved to me. I didn't know her, she didn't know me. *How could she?* To be polite, I nodded.

As I turned away, the door opened and the waitress stepped outside. Short, plump, the apron of her uniform starched and white, she settled against the yellow stucco wall. While she lit a cigarette, she stared at me. Then her eyes lit with recognition.

"You've come home," she said.

I moved next to her. The tag on her blouse said her name was Evelyn. I recalled an Evelyn who'd once worked here. Evelyn Harper had trained as a waitress in this restaurant when I was a kid. *Could this be her?*

That's Niagara Falls, I thought. *The future holds nothing better.*

We chatted until her break was over. As she opened the door, she said, "Stop in for dinner. I'm sure everyone would love to see you."

"Absolutely."

Having made a promise I didn't intend to keep, I walked on.

At the corner, I turned onto Twenty-Third Street. After a couple of blocks, I reached Independence Avenue. This was where I grew up. The house I'd lived in looked much the same. Memories flooded back. My skin tingled. I felt an urge to knock on the door, ask to come in, and climb the stairs to where my bedroom overlooked the tree-lined street. It was a foolish longing. There would be nothing of me in the bedroom. Nothing of my childhood in the house. There never had been.

I stepped back, turned east toward the park and shaded my eyes against the glare of the morning sun. Down the block, a woman on her knees yanked dandelions from a lawn. I gasped. Corrie had been weeding the same lawn the day I left for Manhattan. Like a parched desert nomad, I stumbled toward a mirage of my past, fearful if I blinked it might vanish.

"Corrie Wilder?" I asked, when I drew near. *Why is my heart thumping?*

She tilted her head ever so slightly, and lifted the brim of her straw sunhat. With a laugh, she said, "I haven't been Wilder in a long time."

She shoved her trowel into the lawn, and stood up. Removing her hat, she inspected me. At last, she nodded.

"Richie Morrow. Expensive suit instead of a grunge rock t-shirt, gray at the temples. *Hmm*, you don't look much the worse for wear. Whatever are you doing here?"

She had a few wrinkles around her lips and eyes, and strands of grey highlighted her wheat-blond hair. Yet it seemed as though nothing about Corrie had changed. I'd changed, though. Once I would have stammered, feeling as though she'd pushed me back on my heels. Now, hands on my hips, I mirrored her stance.

"First of all, no one calls me Richie anymore," I said.

Her eyes narrowed. "Oh? What do they call you now?

"People who work for me call me *Mister* Morrow."

"And what do they call you behind your back?"

I shook my head, and smiled. In her presence, it seemed I remembered how to smile.

"Don't know," I said. "They're afraid to let me hear."

"I'll bet."

She lifted her broom. While she swept weeds from the sidewalk, she asked, "And what's second of all?"

"Huh?"

Corrie turned to me, hugging the broom to her chest.

"You said first of all people have fancy things they call you. What's second? Do you intend to stroll back into my life?"

Now I *did* stammer. "Uh… you wrote to me, asked for my help with, uh…" For a moment, I couldn't recall what her letter asked of me.

Her laughter was as melodious as the chirp of sparrows in the nearby birch.

"I'm just tweaking your nose, Richie." She touched my nose. "Still long and straight—how'd you manage not to break it on someone's fist?"

I cleared my throat. "You asked for my help, so I came."

She peered into my eyes. "Didn't have to drop everything, and come all this way. You could've just phoned."

"I could have."

"But, you didn't."

I frowned.

"Well, since you're here, come inside. I'll fix us coffee."

I remembered this house well: post Second World War, wood-frame, two stories—the Wilders lived downstairs, and rented the upstairs apartment to a young couple.

"All these years— With Hal's success, I can't believe you still live in this old place," I said, as we passed through the screen door.

"Why not? It's a *good* house." She looked over her shoulder, as if trying to see the house as I did. "There was a lot of love here."

The living room appeared freshly painted. The sofa and loveseat were covered in bright patterns, the cane-back side chairs wore green enamel. Shadowboxes and abstract paintings filled each wall. At the arch leading to her dining room, she stopped.

"You remember love, don't you, Richie?"

My face grew warm. I looked away. "Don't know what you mean."

"Uh-huh. What was your first wife's name? The second one—do you even remember it? Guess the big city hasn't been as good to you as you hoped."

"Hey, I blew off a dozen appointments to come up here and help an old friend—"

"Who you haven't thought about in a century."

I refused to admit I'd thought of her often over the years. "Don't want my help, say the word. There are plenty of clients ready to pay hefty fees for what I do." I took a few steps toward the front door.

"You still have a temper, I see."

I turned back to her. "You ought to know. You always found a way to bring it out."

She raised her hands in mock surrender, and lowered her eyes. "Thank you for coming."

"That's better." I hung my jacket on the back of the cane rocker.

Over the next couple of hours, and enough coffee to drive me to her bathroom twice, she told me of her life since I left Niagara Falls. After majoring in journalism in college, she'd taken a job with *Art Voice*, a local weekly focused on the culture of Western New York.

"Samuel Clemens lived up here for a while—bet you didn't know that," she said, apropos of nothing.

She was challenging me as she used to, daring me to state I wasn't at all interested in the history—cultural or otherwise—of where I came from. Rather than be drawn into this old argument, I nodded.

When I didn't rise to her bait, Corrie returned to her recollection.

Hal Silvestri had moved to Buffalo after high school. She hadn't seen him again until she was assigned to write a piece on a new exhibit at the Albright-Knox Gallery. As she wandered though one of the halls, deafened by headphones, trying to make sense of the smears and splatters modern artists put on very large canvases, she literally bumped into him. What followed was a minute of apologies. Then Silvestri snatched the headphones, and during the rest of the afternoon, he gave her a live explanation of why this was art. Over dinner, and for the next twenty years, he took pains to explain to her everything he loved about art and literature and theater. He wanted to understand why this area inspired it. Why did people remain here long after the mills and factories relocated? Why did they take even the most menial work so they could remain? Silverstri's search for an answer occupied his thoughts. He painted his questions, and wrote them in his diaries.

"So, what's the answer?" I asked Corrie.

A smile flitted across her face. It was as though she said, if having grown up here I didn't know, her words would be wasted.

She laid her coffee mug on the table, and grabbed her purse and car keys.

"Where are you going?" I asked.

"Not me, us," she said. "If you're going to understand what I want you to do…"

I thought I heard her whisper, *what I* need *you to do*… It was said so softly I couldn't be sure. Before I was able to ask about it, she took my arm.

"There are some things I want you to see."

The first *thing* was about forty minutes from Niagara Falls. Focused on the road, Corrie said little as we exited the Thruway, and shot down Route 219. Just where two counties meet, she slowed and pulled to the shoulder of the road.

I twisted in my seat. "Why are we stopping here?"

"I want to show you this," she said, as she slid from behind the wheel of her pickup.

I followed her to the rail, and leaned over so I could see her face. There were tears in her eyes.

"What?" I asked.

She pointed.

"I don't see anything."

"I know," she said. "That's the problem. You're like so many of the tourists who take photographs of Niagara Falls, but never really see what's before them."

"You're not being fair!"

She slowly shook her head, as if she pitied a poor, benighted fool.

"Open your eyes, Richie."

Instead of pointing, she spread her arms wide.

Beyond the rail, a clear stream gurgled over rocks. Up a steep slope, the lush forest might have stood since receding ice sculpted the mountain. An antlered buck and a doe stopped, and stared down from between two pines. It was as though they asked if I recognized them.

"I brought Hal here," Corrie said. "It became his favorite spot—no fast food restaurants to feed busloads of tourists, just—" She shrugged. "See that dirt road there. A few yards in it becomes a trail climbing over the hill." She glanced at me. "The trail ends in a hollow. Do you remember that hollow, Richie? We used to sneak up there, you and me, and stay overnight in my father's cabin." She grasped my arm. "Do you remember those nights, those days before you ran away?"

"What are you talking about? I never ran away." I stared at her.

She released my arm. "You did! You ran off to Manhattan, and never looked back."

"You know why I went, what I always told you—"

"You told me a lot of things, Richie. You promised to come back in two years."

It was all I could do to keep from laughing. "More than thirty years, and you're still angry about that."

She stepped back, and wiped her eyes on her sleeve. "I'm not angry." She gave a laugh that wasn't really one. "You were what you were."

Staring at the mountain forest I recalled our nights in the hidden cabin, our days roaming among the trees gathering acorns and pine nuts and just… talking. Why had I used Corrie's letter as an excuse to revisit my past—I was certain that's what I'd done. Knowing where my heart was leading me, the wisest thing would be to catch the next plane back to the city, back to clients who asked no more from me than sage advice on how to hide their wealth in overseas accounts. Back to women who would demand no more than social status and eyes which were blind to their affairs. Corrie Wilder was not, would never be such a woman— I stopped in mid-thought. She was Corrie Silvestri now. *Why does that bother me?*

"Hal used to say the light up here is perfect," she was saying when I again focused. "He and I used to come up to the cabin for weeks at a time. Away from everyone."

I gazed around, seeing not the stream or the antlered deer, but the rustic cabin with a wood-burning stove and a simple wood-frame bed in which we, college students yet still children, had cuddled on crisp autumn mornings.

Corrie must have seen something in my eyes. "There's hope for you yet, Richie Morrow." She took my hand, and led me back to her truck. "Now, you can buy me dinner."

***

We stopped at an Irish pub in Lackawanna. *Why here?* I wondered. There were a few fine restaurants in Buffalo and Niagara Falls. We were in a downtrodden area, across a wide street from a General Motors plant. When I left Western New York most of the workers—including my father—had been laid off. The work had been sent south. Some as far south as Mexico. Now the plant's parking lot was full. *A second shift? When did the work come back? Why?* My mind shifted to research I'd ask one of my firm's associates to do. My clients always sought investment opportunities.

Corrie gave me little chance to consider these possibilities. Beer cheese soup, shepherd's pie—lost in talk about the past and people I'd known, it seemed as though in minutes our plates held only scraps. Yet when I glanced at my watch, I saw we'd been there two hours. The only topic we hadn't touched on was Hal Silvestri's foundation. When I broached the subject over Irish coffee, Corrie said she was too weary to think about it. Tomorrow, she said. We'd go through it all then.

She drove home through downtown Buffalo. When I pointed out this wasn't the shortest route, she said there was something else I had to see. She turned onto Forrest

Avenue and pulled to the curb near the sandstone and brick complex that had once been the Buffalo State Asylum for the Insane. I remembered the large building as a wreck: crumbling walls, holes in the floors, deserted towers where ghosts of former inmates were reputed to roam. As teenagers, Corrie and I would sneak in at night, hoping we might see a ghost.

She pointed to construction on the south lawn. "This is just the beginning," she said. "They're renovating the Asylum, going to turn it into a hotel and high-tech conference center."

I felt dumbfounded: the GM plant was alive again, and the ghosts were being exorcised from the lunatic asylum.

When I returned to my hotel room, I stretched out on the bed and telephoned my secretary. I knew she'd still be in the office—nine-to-five is no more than a distant thought at a busy Wall Street law firm.

"Jean," I said, "I'm going to stay through the weekend. Let Mr. Marcus know. Oh, and have one of the associates cover my meeting with the Kushners."

When I left, Western New York had been in its death-throes. If I were to be quite honest, these days it was my heart that had moved someplace else. I froze the thought, and filed it in a hidden part of my mind. I was a businessman. I had to learn how some new Dr. Frankenstein was bringing the area back to life. If there was potential for high returns on investments, I should stay and investigate on behalf of my clients.

The lies one tells oneself.

***

I tossed in bed half the night. I prided myself in spotting possibilities when no one else did. My career had been built on such foresight. *How did I miss the possibilities when I lived here?* Still bothered by my lack of foresight, I rolled over. The bedside clock said it was ten. Sunlight creeping through the window said it was morning. Other Fridays, by ten, I'd have been at my desk for three hours. Most Saturdays, too.

The red light blinked on the telephone. I lifted the receiver, and pushed the button for the hotel operator. "This is Mister Morrow, room four-nineteen," I said, when a nasal voice answered. "There's a message for me?"

"Morrow. Four-nineteen," the voice repeated. "Yes, sir. Mrs. Silvestri phoned, said to have you call her back."

I climbed from the king-sized bed, and stumbled to the bathroom to brush my teeth. It sounds foolish, I realize: though it would be over the telephone, I didn't want to talk to her with morning breath.

"You called?" I said, when Corrie answered.

"Good," she said. "Sylvia got the message right."

"Sylvia?"

"Uh-huh. Sylvia O'Hara. She's been at the Hilton since it opened. You remember her, Richie—she lived in a cottage off Packard Road. She married Eddie Neidermyer—"

"Eddie…?"

"Has old age sapped your memory? You and he were on the high school football team."

While she chatted on about people I hadn't thought of in years, who they married, and how many children they had, I began to feel as though I'd slipped into a time warp. I was again nineteen, and could see their faces, hear their voices. Settled back against the pillows, the phone tucked under my chin, I let Corrie rattle on so as not to lose the warm glow I felt rise from my chest.

"Just listen to me, nattering like my Aunt Phyllis," she said, after what might have been thirty minutes. "I only called to say I've got pancake batter ready for the griddle. How soon can you get here?"

***

Her dining room table was set with dishes of different colors: green cups on blue saucers, white plates, a yellow butter dish.

"Very artistic," I said as I came through the arch dressed in jeans and a long sleeve polo shirt.

"Relax a minute," she called from the kitchen. "Brunch is almost ready."

Five minutes later, she carried in a tray piled with pancakes and bacon. As soon as she put down the tray, her eyes roamed over my outfit, and the slightest smile crossed her lips.

"What?" I said.

Her smile broadened. "Nothing?" She turned on her heels and returned to the kitchen. Immediately she was back with a pot of coffee and a copy of the *Buffalo News*.

"Read this." She laid the paper next to my plate. "Find out what's going on up here."

On the front page was a story about the renovation of the Buffalo State Asylum. The article spoke of how the project would prod a city now yawning and stretching after nearly a half century of sleep. There were golden opportunities here. Green colored opportunities. Damn this woman. I hadn't seen her in thirty years, and she could still read my mind.

"You're still a piece of work," I said, glancing up from the *News*.

Corrie's laugh went from her hazel eyes down to her toes. I'd forgotten how much I enjoyed the sound of her laughter.

When we had eaten, she drove us to the NACC. On the way, I broke into her chatter to ask about the Silvestri Foundation her letter asked me to form. After all, this was the reason I'd come. She ignored my question. With another client, I might grow frustrated and insist he stop wasting my valuable time. To do so with Corrie would have been pointless.

Soon we were atop the concrete stairs at the entrance to what had once been our high school. I yanked at one of the large doors.

"Why are you grunting?" she asked.

"I don't remember these doors being quite so heavy," I said, a little embarrassed.

She pushed me aside. "Age will do that to you." With what appeared to be little effort, she opened the door.

Standing where we had stood so many years before, I felt an ache I hadn't known in years. I couldn't identify the ache… To be honest, I chose not to.

"Are you calling me old?" I said, avoiding where such an untoward thought might lead. The door swooshing closed shoved me into the large entry hall.

"Hey, Corrie. Haven't seen you in a while. Come to check on Hal's work?" a woman said. Lost in Corrie's laughter, I hadn't heard the footsteps or realized anyone was there.

The mention of her husband's name snapped my mind back to where I was, why I had come. Clients waited in Manhattan. I couldn't afford to waste more time.

"Yes… uh, Hal's work," I said. "I really should see—"

At the mentioned of his name, my voice wandered into a jade haze. I forced myself to remember I had no right to be jealous. A long time ago, this woman begged me to stay. I left. Instead of mourning for me, she found someone who shared her love of this corner of New York. This logic failed ease the sting. Seems my heart had logic of its own.

My spine stiffened. *Stop this foolishness,* I thought, *Manhattan is where I belong.*

When my vision cleared, I saw Corrie speaking with the woman who'd approached us. She was thin. Her coal-black hair—obviously dyed—was tied back, and held in place by a paintbrush shoved through a leather loop. Her smock was dotted with paint. The woman pointed at me with her raised chin.

"Is he going to?" she asked.

I'd missed what came before.

Corrie stared past her. "I don't know."

Don't know what? I wanted to ask. But, years of practicing law had taught me to remain silent until I'm certain of the context.

I smiled at the woman. "Richard Morrow," I said.

She took my outstretched hand. "Nice to meet you Richard Morrow. I'm Margaret Hatch."

"Maggie's studio is on the second floor," Corrie said, turning to the woman. "Mind if we stop by? I'd like to show Richie what you're doing." To me, she added, "Hal was her teacher."

"More mentor than teacher," Margaret Hatch said. "Stop by later on." She tilted her shoulders toward the doors to what had once been the school's auditorium. "Right now, I've gotta run. I'm helping with the scenery for the Zack's show."

"Zackary English," Corrie explained. "He's showcasing a new play."

"Up here?" I asked. "Seems a long way from Broadway."

"Not anymore." Margaret frowned.

"Maggie and Zack are newcomers," Corrie said. "Settled here a few years ago. Something about the light, they say." She shrugged as if she had no idea what they meant.

"Not just the light," Margaret said, as she opened the auditorium door. "It's how people who live here see things. Clearer vision."

Speaking of a clear vision," I said, "don't you think it's time we spoke about your husband's estate?"

"Estate?" Margaret said.

Corrie's face turned scarlet.

"Sorry," Margaret whispered, and disappeared into the auditorium.

"What's going on?" I said.

She turned away.

"Corrie?"

"What?"

I heard the sulk in her voice.

"There's no Silvestri Foundation, is there?"

She shook her head.

"No estate to speak of?"

I didn't have to ask the reason for her letter. She'd played me, pulled me from my office, taken me from work which, like a tyrant, commanded my life. She'd stolen my time. *Is this revenge for my lying to her when I promised I'd return?* My face hot, my anger flared in a way it hadn't for years.

"How dare you," I hissed, hands clenched at my sides.

"I just wanted you to come back. I thought if you saw... I don't know what I thought." She knuckled away her tears.

My lips tight, I shoved past her. The door slammed behind me.

***

My mother used to say fate cares little for what one wants. Fate's focus is on what one needs. Though she didn't use those words, it's what she meant.

As if to prove Mom right, all flights to Kennedy Airport were booked. Even my secretary, the resourceful Jean whose mystical powers usually secured anything I asked for, couldn't free-up a ticket. Midnight was the earliest I would be able to leave this godforsaken place. For hours, I paced the Buffalo Airport's corridors, back and forth past shuttered fast food restaurants, past bars closed for the night. I fought to hold onto my anger. As the hours passed, though, I found the task more daunting than calculus.

Corrie Wilder: hair the color of summer wheat. Corrie Wilder who had shoved me into Cheektowaga Creek. Corrie Wilder who still had a talent for making me angrier than I thought possible. Corrie damn Wilder!

I stopped pacing, and stood in front of a tall window, staring at yellow lines on the empty tarmac. After a few minutes, I began to laugh so hard tears formed in my eyes. Soon, my laughter stopped. But, my tears didn't. *How long has it been since I cried, since I laughed, since I felt… anything?*

I turned, and headed for the baggage claim area and the taxi stand beyond. In the cab on my way back to Niagara Falls, I pulled the cell phone from my pocket, and dialed my secretary's home number.

"Sorry to wake you. Things here are far more complicated than I thought. In the morning, tell Mr. Marcus I'm not sure when I'll be back," I said, when Jean answered.

Second Hand

Research teaches a writer all manner of things. Will Deidre remember that some of those things have consequences?

It was a good afternoon for shopping on Worth Street. Ample parking: August, hot, humid, is off-season in West Palm Beach.

Though upscale boutiques sporting *SALE* signs lined both sides of the street, Deidre dodged cars to reach the window of a dimly-lit store. Beyond gilt lettering that read, *WAPINGER'S SECOND HAND*, were vintage dresses on battered seamstress forms, and nineteenth-century hand-tools strewn among a mélange of Art Deco jewelry and partial sets of chipped china. But, Deidre's eyes seemed focused on a rack inside.

Sharon tugged the strap of her cousin's shoulder bag. "You're wasting time." *All the bargains around, you stop here? God, writers are such a pain,* her expression said.

Deidre tilted her head, as if mentally measuring a corner of her living room to determine whether the treasure she'd spotted would fit there.

With a snort, Sharon took half a dozen steps up the block, then stopped. Sighing, she glanced back, turned, and again pulled at her cousin's bag.

"Give me a minute," Deidre complained. A bell tinkled when she opened the door.

Assaulted by the musty odor of things long disused, Sharon halted just inside the shop, sniffed, and sneezed.

Deidre inhaled deeply. She clearly liked the smell of the past.

Another sneeze clogged Sharon's sinuses. She did an about-face. "I'm waiting outside."

The bell rang then rang again. The small relief offered by the shop's overworked air-conditioner was better than the sweltering midday. Braving the musty atmosphere, Sharon craned her neck to peer deep inside. "Now where are you?" Impatiently, she muttered, "Impossible, the way you just disappear—"

"Over here," Deidre called.

"Where?"

Sharon inched down one tight aisle then another, her loose sandals stirring dust from the scarred wood floor.

Deidre was in the third aisle. Crouched on her heels, she flipped the handle of a round-bottomed, cast-iron pot.

"Not another planter? Her house is already a nursery," Sharon complained to the nearby man in an apron.

Wiping perspiration from his forehead that stretched past a fringe of gray hair to the back of his head, the man said to Deidre, "That's an old one. Name's on the bottom near the legs."

Turning the pot on its side, Deidre felt for the stamped-in letters.

"Andre… Verdeau…" The shopkeeper seemed loath to invoke the name.

Deidre looked up at him. Sharon turned away with a head shake and a shrug intended to ask, *Who cares who made that useless thing?*

"Acadian. Ran a foundry upstream from the delta," the shopkeeper said. "1820, 1825, around then."

Deidre nodded.

"Legend has it—"

Sharon's head snapped around. "Not again!"

***

Sharon had seen her cousin go through other passions. Always they ended with a yawned, *It just got old*. Sooner or later everything got old for Deedee—even her marriage to Ray. At least, that's what she'd said, though Sharon knew better. But, her latest mania—for magic, of all things—hadn't abated.

Deidre's fascination with herbalism, and through it, the ability to bend time, nature, human hearts, had begun when she researched a story set in a Louisiana bayou. Her maltreated heroine cast *cunjas*—hexes—for vengeance. She wrote the story just after Ray left her. In a store much like Wappinger's, she'd found a *How Too* on Wicca. The modern emanation of ancient beliefs made sense to her, she'd told Sharon. The universe is interconnected: gravity draws everything to everything else. "It's irrefutably logical," she'd said.

The book outlined herbs which achieved certain results; described the tools needed to cut, mix, and sew the herbs into amulets: silk threads, un-dyed linen, a double-bladed ceremonial knife, colored candles…

It was strange, frightening almost: by following the directions, her cousin seemed able to… well, do things. In fact, Deidre became more adept at it every day. "Nothing evil, mind you," she'd sworn to Sharon. "Evil has… uh, consequences."

So, good things only: an herbal amulet chanted over, and a neighbor's dog that forever threatened Sharon now sought affection from her; another chant and a widower Sharon was mad about called for a date. When she asked, "Did you do that? You didn't… Did you?" Deedee answered with a smile which never failed to annoy, "Does it matter? Got what you wanted."

Not long ago, Deidre had said to reach her desired skill she needed one thing more…

***

𝒟eidre slid the cast-iron bowl from the shelf, and stood up. She turned it, looked inside, and hefted it. "Could be bigger. Still…" she said.

"C'mon already. I can't breathe in here?" Sharon sniffed.

"Stop whining, I'm thinking," Deidre said to her, then, to the shopkeeper, "How much?"

Her lower lip protruding, Sharon clomped to the front of the shop, where she stood, her foot tapping and her hands on her hips, looking out the window.

After a minute, the shopkeeper said, "It's very old... You don't find Verdeau cauldrons everyday... $250?"

"Deedee, come here," Sharon called over her shoulder. "Isn't that Ray's car? Who's the woman with him?"

Deidre's glance lasted only long enough to identify the familiar red Corvette and the blond laughing in the passenger seat. "Marsha... *Blaine*..." She looked up. "Yeah, $250 sounds fine."

Sharon caught her breath. The way her cousin said it...

"Have any black candles?" Deidre asked the shopkeeper. "Two should be sufficient," she said as he headed to the back.

"Oh, no!" Sharon rushed toward her cousin; no sneezes from scattering dust. "No, no, no! You said you'd only... You promised..."

Deidre's smile was inscrutable, her expression unreadable by anyone who knew her less well than Sharon.

Kaddish

Understanding takes time; sometimes considerable time. As Susan recalls her mother's death in the Jewish traditions of *Shiva* and the period during with *Kaddish* is recited each morning and evening, she begins to learn who she is and where she comes from.

Pellets of snow stung my cheeks. I bent into the January wind, and reached for my brother's arm. He glanced at me from the corner of his eye. For a moment I thought he might brush my hand from his sleeve.

"It was nice," I said.

Linda, his wife of three years, leaned across him. "What was?"

"What the rabbi said about Mom." My chest tingled as I recalled the eulogy. "The only time she made her family cry was when she died—that was nice, wasn't it, Robby?"

"Robert," my brother corrected me in a voice as stiff as his shoulders. He stroked his moustache, then flicked snowflakes from his black hair, so flecked with gray it belied his age. Next month he would be forty-three.

"It *was* nice," Linda said. She pulled her knit hat so low over her ears she nearly knocked the glasses from her small nose.

"I suppose," Robert said. "But, he didn't know her." He drew his coat tight around his broad frame. "For a few bucks, he probably says the same thing about everyone."

"I wish Phil were here," I said. "He knew Mom." Rabbi Bentley and his wife, Deborah, were old friends.

Robert shrugged. Who officiated at our mother's funeral made little difference to him. It wasn't that he didn't love Mom—he and Linda had cared for her, seen to her every need during the nine months cancer gnawed at her lungs. But, for my brother, this rite—anything to do with religion—was merely to be endured.

"At least the guy kept it short." He shook my hand from his arm, and wound his scarf around his neck.

Linda frowned at him. "Did you remember to ask the rabbi to come over and lead the prayer tonight?"

"Did you?" I said.

His eyes straight ahead, Robert's lips tightened. It was as though I'd accused him of a breach of etiquette.

We were walking along the narrow road cutting through the heart of the old cemetery. To the left and right paths bent off, curled around a city of mausoleums, and ran through arches erected by burial societies named for the *shtetls*—the villages in Eastern Europe—in which our grandparents had been born. Beyond the arches were tall headstones which in the spring would be adorned by neat flower beds.

At the end of the road we passed through an iron gate, and into the chapel's parking lot. I waved goodbye to my two surviving aunts and the cousins who'd braved the snow, and dropped my eyes when I received no more than half-hearted nods in return. This was the price of being the family outcast.

With a sigh, I pulled a set of keys from my purse. As I unlocked the door of my car, I called to my brother, "Is there anything we need? I can stop at the market on the way."

We would sit *shiva* at Robert's house, and I suspected he might not have bought enough food and drink for the relatives and friends who would stop by in the next seven days to share memories of our mother. Hosting this ritual wasn't my brother's choice: our father had passed away two years ago, so the obligation for *shiva* and gathering with a minion of nine other men to say *Kaddish*—the Jewish prayer for the dead—was wrapped as tight as the scarf around his neck. He was the only son.

"We've got plenty," Linda said.

"And people always bring food," Robert added, then muttered, "As if I can't afford to feed them."

Linda smacked his arm.

"Okay, then," I said, "I'll just stop at home to get what I baked."

They didn't hear me. My brother's car was already exiting the lot.

***

The large colonial house in Roslyn Heights was by no means a mansion. Still, it announced to passersby a successful man dwelt within. My brother had become what my parents wished for their children. I, on the other hand, had been unable to do something as simple as make a marriage work.

What might have been a full stadium parking lot greeted me when I turned onto Robert's street. Even his circular drive was jammed. A quick glance informed me my eight-year-old Saturn wouldn't fit into the only small space, so I parked around the corner. Balancing two trays of noodle pudding—when I was a child, Mom had taught me Grandma's *kugel* recipe—and fighting a wind that tried to rip off my coat, I made my way down the block. When I opened the front door, it seemed as though I'd walked into a cocktail party.

I saw no torn lapels, no covered mirrors or crates to sit on. I heard no soft-spoken remembrances of a woman's life well-lived. Instead, laughter pealed from the large square living room, dining room, down the hall and up the stairs. Bottles clinked on glasses. Someone was playing the piano. My brother had made this an Irish wake.

Robert circled the corner from his den. He'd changed from his suit into a tan corduroy jacket, jeans, and oxblood penny loafers. His cheeks were red—they would get that way after only two drinks. He glanced at the trays in my hand. He glanced at my old wool overcoat. Speaking to the glass of tequila in his hand, he said, "Glad you could make it, big sister." He didn't reach out to take the trays I held.

Had I the desire, or at the moment the strength to point out his ill manners, he would have claimed he was being ironic. My brother had difficulty differentiating irony from sarcasm. He hadn't always been this way. It's just that he had little tolerance for failure, and a failure was how he viewed me since my divorce.

Mom had also thought me a failure—with good reason, I supposed. "You and Ron can work it out," she'd told me the day I showed up at her house, suitcase in hand. "Your father and I always worked things out," she'd told me each time I visited her at Robert's house during her illness. Tied to a marriage which had gone sour, I had an affair, and moved out. The judge gave my ex custody of our daughter. Mom was again terribly disappointed in me, embarrassed in front of her friends. It had never been different: I'd been a hippy in college, a rebel, a nomadic wild-child disappearing who knew where, sleeping with who knew whom, and getting arrested in Birmingham and in Chicago. "No wonder you can't get along with your husband," she'd told me.

I'd lost my temper then. "Guess people are right when they talk about the apple and the tree," I'd snapped. "After all, you named me for Dad's great-aunt, and she got burned by the Tsar's army for causing trouble."

Unlike my brother, I recognized sarcasm when it bounced out of my mouth. I'd heard Mom crying when I stormed out my brother's house a few weeks before she died. Though he never said it, I'm sure Robert blamed me for our mother's death—he believed I was the reason she refused treatment which might extend her life by maybe a year.

Nights I sat alone in my apartment, I blamed me, too.

***

Linda emerged from the kitchen. A green apron covered the black dress she'd worn to the funeral. Her neck-length hair, the color of autumn hay, was now tied back. She glared at Robert. "Let me take those, Susan," she said to me.

My brother's eyes now rested on a color photograph hung on the wall. It was taken outside a bed and breakfast on Martha's Vineyard just after his wedding. My ex and I were in the picture. From the expression on Robert's face and way he pulled at his mustache when he looked at the picture, he might have been telling our parents he only put up with me for their sake.

Linda took one of the trays and my arm. "Give me a hand in the kitchen, would you?" She turned her back on her husband.

In contrast to the heavy overcast outside, the kitchen was bright: white from cupboards to appliances. Beyond the windows and French doors, under an inch or two of snow, what appeared to be an acre of lawn was ready for the children my sister-in-law hoped to have one day. I couldn't help but compare her life to the miniature one I led in the basement efficiency apartment I inhabited.

"I apologize for my husband, Sue," she said.

"No need to." I gave her a smile that wasn't really one. "I've known him a long time."

Robert's voice barged through the kitchen door: "We need more food out here."

Linda shook her head. "All those years you grew up together, and you didn't kill him?"

I laughed. "Well, there was one time I tried to plug his finger into a socket."

Her brow furrowed, she stared at me as though she were uncertain whether I was serious.

"I might have done it if Mom hadn't heard him crying."

"Why'd you do that?"

I pointed to the bend where my nose had been broken. "He threw a block from his playpen. Hit me right here. Mom rushed to him, and left me sitting with a bloody nose."

Robert interrupted my resentment: "How about some food?"

"Better get the platters out there," Linda said. "Drinking on an empty stomach, he's liable to throw a block at *me*."

I poked my head through the door, and peered around the living room at the bodies on plush sofas and chairs, at the feet up on the glass tables. "I don't see any of our relatives here. Where's Aunt Florence? Aunt Millie?"

"They said they'll stop by another time. Rob's business people wanted to come today to pay their respects. They all have to work tomorrow."

I heard a glass shatter.

"Nothing to worry about," Robert called. "I'll clean it up."

"Yeah," I said. "I can see their respects."

Linda shrugged. "What can I say—car salesmen."

For the next hour we carried food into the dining room and empty platters into the kitchen. It seemed only minutes before a garbage bag was filled with the empty bottles I hauled to the trash cans outside.

When I slammed the lid on one of the cans, the wind crept up and encircled me. As if the ghost of my past stood at my back, I felt a tingle at the nape of my neck. Or maybe my mother stood there. But that couldn't be, it was Robert she would have gone to. So maybe it was Grandma. On Sabbath evenings at her kitchen table, it was she who patiently taught me what I knew of my heritage. Through the years, in all my wanderings, I'd felt her beside me.

I stopped and laughed at the idea. I'd grown too old for such foolish notions.

As I stepped aside to return to the house, the tingling in my neck spread downward. The wind touched my hand. It was almost a caress. With a shiver, I gazed at the sky. The fiery orange of a setting sun broke through the gray cloud cover. The sight pulled me back to my teenage Fridays in Brooklyn, to Grandma lifting the shade to peek through her window. I could almost hear her say, "Sun's down. *Shenah maideleh—*" my little one, she'd always called me in Yiddish "—light the candles."

I wrapped my arms around my chest. Though Grandma had left me her candlesticks, I hadn't lit Sabbath candles in years. I'd forgotten how to pray. But now, held by the memory, I whispered the Sabbath blessing of the candles: "*Baruch atah adonai—*"

The wind drifted away. I stood, as if frozen.

"Susan?" Linda leaned out the back door.

I didn't move, didn't even turn my head to look in her direction.

She came outside and touched my arm. "You okay?"

I nodded slowly.

"You'll catch a cold," she said. "Come inside. The rabbi just got here—they're gonna say *Kaddish*."

***

Robert's den was oak-paneled, and lined with bookshelves. He was a reader. History: his primary interest was the Civil War. He also had sections of books on Western Europe and the Orient. I found it interesting that nothing in his library told of Russian Poland—the place our family fled just before the First World War.

Instead of a quiet place to read, that evening the den was crowded. More than a dozen men leaned on the teakwood desk and against the walls, and lounged in the leather chairs. My brother was at the window, staring out.

Several women blocked the doorway, whispering to each other.

"I wonder what this is about," one said.

"Do you think they'll say the prayer in English?" her friend asked.

"I hope so. My mother told me to be careful—you never can tell what someone might make you say."

"Might even be a sin."

Clearly, these women weren't Jewish. Neither, I suspected, were many of the men. Still, I appreciated the fact they'd risk their immortal souls by praying in Hebrew for my mother.

The rabbi rested his briefcase on the floor, and pulled out a blue felt bag decorated with yellow stripes and a Star of David. From this bag, he took his *tallis*—his prayer shawl—kissed the hem, and draped it around his neck. Again he reached into his briefcase. This time he came out with a sheaf of pages he distributed to the men.

I took Linda's arm. "Come on."

She shook her head. In the orthodox tradition she'd been born to, this prayer was to be said only by men.

I pushed past the women at the door, and put my hand out to the rabbi.

He tried to ignore me by looking at the pages he held. These had both the Hebrew version and a large-type transliteration of the *Kaddish*.

"She was my mother, too," I told him.

He glanced at my brother.

Robert shrugged.

At last, the rabbi handed me a page, and again ignored me as he counted the men. Apparently he thought God wouldn't hear us unless ten *men* chanted the words. Satisfied, he glanced around the den.

"For those of you who aren't familiar with our customs," he said, "this is the prayer we say for our departed. It's interesting to note that nowhere in this prayer do we speak of death. Instead we talk of the glory of God whose wisdom and strength we can't approach. Now, in memory of…" He looked to Robert.

Before my brother could answer, I said, "Jeanne— our mother's name is Jeanne."

"Yes, um," the rabbi said. "In memory of Jeanne, please read along with Robert."

I glared at him. "And Susan."

"Uh, yes. Of course. Please read along with Robert … and Susan. *Yisgadal v'yistkadash shmay rabbah…"* He looked abound, then translated, "Glorified and sanctified is God's name."

Stumbling over the strange words, the men read the prayer.

I glanced at Robert. Still peering out the window, as if he saw Mom standing in the snow, he repeated only every third word. And those he said were a beat behind the rabbi. If he really saw Mom, perhaps he was apologizing to her for his discomfort with our customs. Nights I'd sat with Grandma learning who I am, he'd watched television with Dad.

"Oleyu v'al kol yisro-eyl," the rabbi intoned, *"v'imru omeyn."*

"Amen," I said.

In the brief silence that followed, one of the women at the den door clapped.

I glared at her.

She blushed, and stepped back into the hall.

While the rabbi gathered his pages, Robert went to his desk and wrote the man a check. I didn't know why, but instead of returning my copy of the prayer, I folded it in eighths and shoved it in the pocket of my skirt.

When I rolled over in bed to turn off the alarm the next morning, my hand settled on the page I'd placed on the night table. Instead of my routine of reading a novel in bed until my eyes closed, I'd sat up reading the prayer over and over. As when I pocketed the page in my brother's den, I didn't know why. Maybe it was because, while I recited the prayer along with the rabbi last evening, Grandma reached out and touched my hand. Stranger things have happened. For whatever reason, sometime around midnight

I reached a decision: I knew Robert wouldn't go to the synagogue each morning and evening for the next year to recite *Kaddish*, so I'd say it. Then, remembering the rabbi's disdain of my audacity for daring to be part of his minion, I reached another decision: I would recite it alone at home. I didn't know if this would count for anything, but I'd do it just the same.

Why?

I had an answer to *this* question: guilt is part of *my* tradition.

***

Each morning before putting on my makeup, even before having my first cup of coffee, and every evening after sundown, I turned to the east. I turned east because Grandma had told me in the old-country *shul* where my forebears worshipped—a two-story wooden edifice not grand enough to be called a synagogue—a seat against the eastern wall was considered an honor. I'd never asked her why, yet thought it had to mean something. So, I turned east, and read aloud, *"Yisgadal v'yistkadash shmay rabbah—"*

I wish I could say it was easy to remain true to my intention. It wasn't. Too much temptation.

In July, women I worked with came into my office near the end of the day. "We're going down to Rosie O'Grady's for drinks after work," they said. "Wanna come?"

My mouth watered. At the mere suggestion, I tasted the creaminess of the Guinness Stout I usually ordered. More, I tasted a desire for the broad shouldered men around the horseshoe bar, who would gladly buy me a pint or two, then suggest we find a quiet place for dinner. And maybe a night making love afterward.

I gulped back the almost uncontrollable urge, and forced my eyes down to the papers on my desk. "Sorry...

can't," I said. "Gotta get this contract done by Thursday. I'll be here for hours. Another time?"

Why couldn't I tell them I had to get home to pray for my mother? They might have understood. Or they might have gone off to Rosie's giggling, and told the crowed bar, "Susan's gone religious on us."

Five minutes after they left my office, I closed my file, turned off my computer, and rode the elevator down to the street. I turned my face as I passed Rosie's windows so my coworkers wouldn't spot me and know I'd lied.

After a month of *another times* they stopped asking me to join them.

This didn't make it easier, though. In September my friend Janet's brother moved back east. His divorce was final. He asked about me. Richard—Ricky—and I had dated all through high school. It seemed he wanted to reach out to his past.

"C'mon," Janet said to me on the phone. "It'll be fun. We can double-date like we used to."

I remembered Ricky. Too well. He'd been the star pitcher on the school's baseball team, a member of the honor society, and a hell of a lay. He'd been my first. Then he left for college in Los Angeles. Had I searched for the Elysian time with him though all these years and dozens of relationships that didn't last?

"Sorry, Jan, can't," I told her. "There's, um… something I've gotta do."

"What's so important you can't put it off till tomorrow?" she asked.

I wouldn't tell her, either.

At my next session with my shrink—after my divorce I'd thought it was time I learned why I found it hard to settle down—I asked why I couldn't tell anyone I was saying *Kaddish* morning and night.

She smiled as if she knew a secret. "Isn't the more pertinent question why you're doing it?"

I bristled. "Okay, tell me why."

"Why do *you* think that is?"

Damn! Would I have asked if I knew the answer?

After an hour of talking around the issue—and trying hard to change the subject—I went home and lit a joint. Maybe the answer would come to me if I got stoned.

After another session with my shrink in October, I opened my night table and reached for my stash. I stared through the plastic baggie at the pot and rolling papers within. For the first time in months, years, I had no taste for it. I put the baggie back and closed the drawer.

It wasn't until early December that the answer to why I said *Kaddish* every day came to me. And I literally mean it came to me.

On Long Island, the late autumn sun doesn't begin to rise in the morning until past seven. It was a Saturday—I remember the day because, no need to catch an early train to Manhattan, I was able to sleep in. Around six, I was awakened by a stirring in my basement efficiency. Maybe it was a breeze rustling the documents I'd brought home from my office to work on over the weekend. I was about to roll toward the wall, punch my pillows, and fight to return to whatever I'd been dreaming, when my mind cleared enough that I realized there could be no breeze in my room. It was near freezing outside; my windows were closed and locked. Then what caused the papers to flutter? Perhaps I *had* left a window open. I rolled onto my side and opened one eye.

In the center of my room I saw a flash of bright light—not yellow and orange like in a flame, this was all white, an absence of color. As if a flashbulb had gone off, the light blinded me.

I snapped my eyes shut and rubbed them. The light still flashed behind my lids. What was going on in my apartment? Was… I being robbed? My stomach began to churn.

Trembling, I again opened one eye, this time just a slit.

The light still filled the center of the room, and now it fluttered as though it were a candle kissed by a gentle breeze.

"What the—" I muttered, my voice rasping with fear.

I tried to pull my quilt over my head, but I couldn't move.

The fluttering became more pronounced. While I watched, a figure walked slowly into the light. It was a woman, her dark hair and her dress blown as if by a gale wind. She turned. I saw her face.

I blinked rapidly.

This… was my mother.

"Thank you," she said, although I'm not sure if her voice was just in my mind. "I'm all right now. Tell Linda." She waved, smiled, turned, and walked into the center of the light, growing smaller with each step until she was gone. The light flickered, went out. My room was bathed in darkness.

"Ma!" I cried, my arms outstretched.

Silence answered me.

I peered into the darkness, craving another sight of her. Leaning on an elbow, I continued to search the shadows in the corners until my eyes grew heavy, blinked, then closed.

***

I woke to sunlight streaming through my windows. I brushed my teeth, put up coffee. I pulled from a drawer the wrinkled sheet on which the transliteration of *Kaddish* was typed. I turned to the east, and read, "*Yisgadal v'yistkadash shmay rabbah—*"

The prayer completed, I replaced the folded page in the draw, and sat at the table with my coffee and the newspaper. On the wall to my left was the red and polished-wood baker's rack on which I stored my dishes. Beyond that was the nook in which I slept. To my right was a high window looking out on the motorcycle parked in a neighbor's driveway. Had this been a Sunday before my divorce, I would have phoned my mother from the dinette in a three bedroom split level house so we could do the crossword puzzle together. At the memory of those days before I was an outcast, tears filled my eyes. Feeling sorry for myself, as I idly brushed my fingers across the newspaper the dream I had returned. I recalled a light, blindingly bright, filling my room. The vision was as clear as this crisp December day. Mom was in the center of the light. She thanked me, waved goodbye. My chest fluttering as the light had, I broke into sobs. Never had I had a dream so achingly clear and well-remembered past my first cup of morning coffee.

But… was it a dream? Had my mother returned, however briefly, to tell me something?

Nonsense! I knuckled away my tears. This was reality, not a restaging of a scene from *Fiddler on the Roof.*

Yet it had seemed so real… I glanced at the drawer holding the printed prayer.

Ridiculous! I told myself. I shoved the newspaper and the dream aside, thinking, *Time to get on with the day.*

Still, while I carried my clothes to the Laundromat, did my marketing in Walbaums, and wandered through the Mid-Island Mall in search of a new blouse, the dream I tried to convince myself wasn't one, returned again and again. Maybe that was it: I didn't want it to have been just a dream. I'd wanted to see my mother one more time, wanted again to feel part of her. Wanted her to stroke my hair as she'd done when I was a child, and utter words of comfort. She had told me something, though: *I'm all right now. Tell Linda.*

For a message from beyond, what Mom said was just so… mundane! So, it had to be a dream.

As I emerged from a store in the mall with a plastic bag in my hand, shoppers stared when I stopped and roughly wiped away tears.

See, Susan? I thought. *The answer becomes clear if you just reason it out.*

My careful logic failed to make anything clear. Through dinner, what I had seen early that morning sat in the chair next to me. I couldn't shake the feeling my mother had actually told me something I needed to know. Or do. Yes, she'd told me to tell Linda what I saw. Maybe Linda would know what Mom wanted me to understand.

At last, my single place setting cleared and the dishes washed, I phoned my sister-in-law.

"I don't know what this is supposed to mean," I said as soon as she answered the phone. "But… uh…" I felt as foolish as my brother and mother believed me to be. Had I been staring in a mirror, I would have seen my face grow red from my neck to my forehead.

"Is something the matter?" she asked.

"No, no. It's not that."

"If something's wrong, I can come right over."

Someone cared I might be in pain—was this what Mom wanted me to know?

"No, Linda, nothing's wrong," I said. "It's just that … well, I had a… dream."

Stammering, I told her how I'd been awaken by a stirring, and been blinded by a glow in the center of my room. Again my eyes were clouded by tears. "Anyhow, Mom asked me to tell you she's all right now." I tried to laugh, as if I knew how silly I sounded.

There was no laughter on the other end of the line. I heard Linda gasp, and begin to cry. "Thank you," she said. "Thank you… Susan." She hung up.

Okay, I thought as I put down the phone, *it wasn't just a dream. I did what Mom asked. I can put it behind me, now.*

Except I couldn't. Like a dramatized movie adaptation of a scene from someone's biography, what I'd seen and heard now had a life of its own.

On Monday, work was a waste. Time and again my mind returned to my mother's words. *It had to mean more than telling Linda she's okay,* I thought. But, it didn't. Did it?

At three o'clock, pleading illness I left the office. About the time the Long Island Railroad reached the Jamaica station, I decided to call my shrink. Maybe she could explain the dream. Between Jamaica and Syosset, I decided I had no patience for another question smashed back at me like a tennis ball. So, instead of my shrink I phoned my friend, Deborah, the rabbi's wife. She was the one person I'd told what I was doing; the one person I knew wouldn't laugh at me.

I spoke quickly, the way I do when I don't want to be interrupted by someone asking if I were stoned. When I finally took a breath, Deborah remained silent.

"You still there?" I asked—a foolish question, since I heard her breathing.

After a minute, which felt far longer, she said, "This might not have been a dream."

"It… it might not have been…"

"Uh-uh." She inhaled, probably a drag from a cigarette. "When did your mother die?"

"January ninth," I said. "Why?"

I heard another inhalation. "And today's December eleventh. So, this happened on the morning of the ninth."

"Yeah. So? What does that mean?"

It sounded as though she exhaled her cigarette smoke. "You're finished saying *Kaddish.*"

"No," I said. "It's not a year yet."

"Yes."

"But, the rule is—"

"Yes," she said again.

I yanked back my hair. If my shrink had batted the question back at me, it might have been easier than this conversation with Deborah. I felt as though I were spinning. "I don't understand."

"Our rule is to say *Kaddish* for a year. But, there's also tradition. And by tradition, we stop after eleven months. It's our way of telling God your mother was such a good person she didn't need a full year."

I caught my breath. I hadn't known of this. When Grandma died, I never counted the months my father went to his synagogue after dinner. When Dad died, Mom paid a rabbi to say *Kaddish*. Robert hadn't spoken the prayers for Mom. So, this meant… could what I'd seen have been real?

Deborah and I spoke for a few more minutes. To this day, I have no idea what we said. I was crying.

Now I understood why my mother had come to me—whether or not it was in a dream didn't matter. And I also at last understood the true reason I'd prayed each morning and evening. Laying my selfish desires aside for eleven months, every evening and morning I'd begged her forgiveness. I had been a difficult child, a more difficult adult. I had yanked at her heart more times than she ever allowed me to see. And even after she was gone, she returned—I desperately wanted what I'd seen to have been real—to say I was forgiven.

On my bed, with my knees pulled up to my chin, I cried until after sunset. I was alone in a basement efficiency apartment. There was no one to blame for this but me. Perhaps it was time I forgave myself.

***

Mom's been gone sixteen years, yet the morning she came to me is still as present as my memory of her face and her voice. Was it a dream? Was it really her in the blinding light? I'll never know. Does it matter?

Some things have changed for me through the years: these days I feel more settled, and don't seek fast times in strange beds. I volunteer my time where I can—most recently lighting Grandma's candles while I lead Sabbath services in an old age home. And I write. Quiet evenings at my computer, I record my memories of who I am and where I came from. Perhaps this is a sign that at last, like Robert, I've become the person Mom hoped I'd be.

Yet, as I write this, I realize not all the hurts I've caused are healed. Typing the words my mother spoke early one December morning, I find a tacit message hidden in them. That message begs a question, so simple yet after all these years, difficult to answer. Difficult, because I'm still alone. I wasn't able to reconcile with my ex, and my daughter and I— I've torched too many bridges.

So, this unspoken question presses on my mind now that I'm nearing the age Mom was: who will say *Kaddish* for me?

About the Author:

Formerly a Manhattan entertainment attorney and a contributing editor to the quarterly art magazine SunStorm Fine Art, Susan Lynn Solomon now lives in Niagara Falls, New York, where she is in charge of legal and financial affairs for a management consulting firm.

After moving to Niagara Falls she became a member of Just Buffalo Literary Center's Writers Critique Group, and since 2009 many of of her short stories have appeared in literary journals, including, *Abigail Bender* (awarded an Honorable Mention in a Writer's Journal short romance competition), *Ginger Man, The Memory Tree, Elvira, Going Home, Yesterday's Wings,* and *Sabbath* (nominated for *2013 Best of the Net* by the editor of *Prick of the Spindle*).

Her latest short stories are Reunion, about an individual who must face family after undergoing a transgender operation, appeared in a recent issue of *Flash Fiction Press, Captive Soul,* which was included in Solstice Publishing's Halloween anthology, *Now I Lay Me Down To Sleep, Volume 1,* and *Niagara Falling,* about a man returning to his hometown, which was written for the Solstice Publishing anthology, *Adventures in Love.*

Susan Lynn Solomon's Solstice Publishing novel, The Magic of Murder, is available now. *Voices In My Head* is the first collection her short stories.

Acknowledgements:

Most of the stories in this book were presented to the Just Buffalo Literary Writers' Critique Group, and would not have taken the form they have today without the thoughtful comment offered by the incredibly talented writers who are member of that group. Specifically I want to thank the group's moderator, Gary Earl Ross, an Edgar

Award winning playwright and author, for time and patience while going through many of the stories including in Voices In My Head, and helping to and for his constant encouragement. I also must acknowledge Jerome Gentes, another talented writer and poet and the group's former moderator for his patient suggestions in connection with *Mystery of the Carousel* and *Thieves Game*. In this regard, I also thank Frederick Crook, author of a number of novels, for reading and commenting on *Mystery of the Carouse*l and encouraging me to include it in this volume.

With great gratitude, I thank Solstice Publishing for believing in my first novel, *The Magic of Murder*, and in my short stories and I thank the marvelous family of Solstice writers—many of whom have become friends—for so generously sharing their experiences. Finally, I thank Kc Sprayberry for accepting this collection and shepherding through the editing and publication process, and I thank Debbie Rowe, my editor for this volume for her patience in going through each work and helping to pull everything together.

Social Media Links:

Website: http://www.susanlynnsolomon.com/

Facebook: https://www.facebook.com/susanlynnsolomon

LinkedIn: https://www.linkedin.com/in/susan-solomon-8183b129

If you like this book, check out Susan Lynn Solomon's other Solstice Publishing novel:

The Magic of Murder

When his partner is discovered in a frozen alley with eight bullets in his chest, Niagara Falls Police Detective Roger Frey swears vengeance. But Detective Chief Woodward has forbidden him or anyone else on the detective squad to work the case. Emlyn Goode knows Roger will disobey his boss, which will cost him his job and his freedom. Because she cares for him more than she'll admit, she needs to stop him. Desperate, she can think of but one way.

Emlyn recently learned she's a direct descendent of a woman hanged as a witch in 1692. She has a book filled with arcane recipes and chants passed down through her family. Possessed of, or perhaps by a vivid imagination, she intends to use these to solve Jimmy's murder before Roger takes revenge on the killer. But she's new to this "witch thing," and needs help from her friend Rebecca Nurse, whose ancestor also took a short drop from a Salem tree. Also in the mix is a rather hefty albino cat (Elvira detests being called fat). Rebecca's not much better at deciphering the ancient directions, and while the women and the cat stumble over spell after spell, the number of possible killers grows. They'd better quickly come up with a workable spell: when Chief Woodward's wife is shot and a bottle bomb bursts through Emlyn's window, it becomes clear she's next on the killer's list.

http://bookgoodies.com/a/B015OQO5LO